The feel of her sm**d him eradicated mind. The reaso fact that he was deceiving her and** **no intention of allowing the show to continue—everything wiped out. Clean.**

Hell, he would have a hard time remembering his own name he was so stunned by her reaction.

Without conscious thought or will he drew back and lifted her face, forcing her chin up and making her look at him.

"And I think it's time we drop the formality. My name is Keanu. Friends call me Key," he said, brushing a finger beneath her chin and tilting her face farther up so he could see her eyes.

Her throat constricted as she swallowed, biting her lower lip in obvious nervousness, a gesture he'd seen her do on more than one occasion. His eyes followed the trail of her small tongue.

"And can we be that?" she said, her voice husky. "Friends?"

"Yes," he said, hearing the deepness in his own voice, but not giving a damn. "I think we can be that. At least," he finished, his eyes locked on hers.

Her startled gaze was centered on him, and as he leaned down and brought their faces together, bringing their mouths into alignment, he slanted his mouth over hers.

Books by Kimberly Kaye Terry

Harlequin Kimani Romance

Hot to Touch
To Tempt a Wilde
To Love a Wilde
To Desire a Wilde
To Have a Wilde

KIMBERLY KAYE TERRY'S

love for reading romances began at an early age. Long into the night she would stay up with her night-light on until she reached "the end," praying she wouldn't be caught reading what her mother called "those" types of books. Often she would acquire her stash from beneath her mother's bed. Ahem. To date she's an award-winning author of seventeen novels in romance, paranormal romance and erotic romance, and has garnered acclaim for her work. She happily calls writing her full-time job…after chauffeuring around her teenage fashionista daughter, that is.

Kimberly has a bachelor's degree in social work and a master's degree in human relations and has held licenses in social work and mental health therapy in the United States and abroad. She and her daughter volunteer weekly at various social service agencies and she is a long-standing member of Zeta Phi Beta Sorority, Inc., a community-conscious organization. Kimberly is a naturalist and practices aromatherapy. She believes in embracing the powerful woman within each of us and meditates on a regular basis. Kimberly would love to hear from you. Visit her at www.kimberlykayeterry.com.

To Have a
WILDE

Kimberly Kaye Terry

H HARLEQUIN® KIMANI™ ROMANCE

This book is dedicated to
my wonderful daughter, Hannah, aka "junior"...
you are simply the best; 'nuff said ;)

Recycling programs
for this product may
not exist in your area.

ISBN-13: 978-0-373-86312-9

TO HAVE A WILDE

Copyright © 2012 by Kimberly Kaye Terry

For questions and comments about the quality of this book please contact us at CustomerService@Harlequin.com.

HARLEQUIN®
www.Harlequin.com

Printed in U.S.A.

Dear Reader,

I am thankful for the opportunity to bring to you the fourth book in my Wilde family saga, *To Have a Wilde*. Writing Keanu "Key" Kealoha and Sonia Brandon's story has been an adventurous and wonderful ride for me! These two characters touched me in new ways, making me fall in love with their story even before I began to write it. Their story is emotional at times, comical at others, and at all times hot and sexy...just the way we like it! The fireworks between these two very strong-willed characters are ignited from the start, and the flames of passion are threaded throughout, until the smoking-hot ending. Key and Sonia took me from boardroom clashes to lazy days on the ranch, and to the bedroom, where the flames of heat and desire blazed even hotter. I truly hope you enjoy reading Sonia and Key's story as much as I enjoyed writing it.

Thank you to everyone who has emailed me and told me how much you have enjoyed reading about my Wilde boys...and fussed at me for taking so long to write the next one. I hope *To Have a Wilde* makes up for it. As always, thank you for the support and love, and I will continue to do my best to write hot, sexy and exciting stories featuring alpha men and the women they love!

As always, be good, my wonderful readers. If not, be delicious in your naughty. Whichever works best for you. Whatever you do, keep it sexy. ;)

KKT

Chapter 1

Shouldering an arm against the heavy wooden door to open it, the only thing on Keanu "Key" Kealoha's mind after a grueling day wrestling, branding and working cattle was getting intimate with a warm, willing woman.

He ran a hand through his hair, spiking the long-ish inky-black strands over his head as he tiredly walked his horse into the massive stable. It was time for a damn haircut, he thought.

He dropped his hand from his head and allowed it to rest on the thick, corded-muscled back of the stallion as he strode farther inside with the animal.

Frustration with just about everything, hair included, was riding him as hard as he'd just ridden the horse. He gave the animal a consoling, swift pat.

But not nearly as hard as he wanted...scratch that, *needed*...to ride a woman. And not just any woman would do. The image of who he wanted beneath him rolled into his mind.

As if the *thought* had the right to take up residence in his mind. As though he'd given *her* the right.

As soon as the accompanying image entered his thoughts, Key growled low in his throat.

The mental images and thoughts pissed him off more than the past twenty-four hours had. And after the past twenty-four hours he'd had, he could do without them.

His mind still reeled, spinning the information over and over, thinking of what he'd learned...and *how* he would tell his brother.

He shook his head, blowing out a disgusted breath. He shelved that problem to another part of his brain for later contemplation.

He had enough on his plate as it was. There was no time to wonder how he was going to figure out how to deal with the skeleton in his family closet he'd recently discovered and what it meant for him and Nick.

Finding out what his mother had done was hard enough for him to swallow. The fact that he and Nick weren't their father's biological sons was something that hurt like hell. Not that he and Nick hadn't always suspected they weren't the biological sons of Alek Kealoha, the man who raised them.

But to see in black-and-white, in the form of his

mother's personal letters he'd found, which chronicled her life from the time she was a young woman to her death, and what he'd learned, was something else entirely.

He sighed. In actuality, it was something he and his brother had talked about for years, the suspicion that Alek wasn't their natural father, but because they loved him unconditionally, they'd mutually agreed to shelve the discussion. Permanently.

Although they resembled their mother, their blue eyes had always been a source of question. But neither his mother nor father ever spoke about it, even though others never seemed to have a hard time gossiping about it. Not that he or Nick had ever suffered because of it. Despite their lack of resemblance to their father, their family had been tight-knit.

Yet he felt a rising anger at his mother's duplicity and felt guilty as hell. And the fact that he had been the one to go through her personal things had been a given.

Throughout her illness, it had been made obvious to Key that his father wouldn't be able to handle that task after her death. He was too close to her, loved her too much to deal with the pain. As for Nick…no way was his twin going to do it. Key had been told *that* in no uncertain terms.

There was no one else, and Key had shouldered the responsibility.

As Key had begun the cheerless task of sorting

through his mother's belongings, he'd stumbled upon her diary.

Really, calling it a diary was a stretch. It was a collection of…letters.

At first glance, Key had seen the letters, bundled together and tied with a satin bow, and thought them love letters between his parents, and had set them aside for his father to peruse, not wanting to read something he thought to be intimate exchanges between his parents.

When he'd seen another man's name on one letter, his hand paused in the act of placing them aside. Despite his inner voice telling him he didn't need to tread there…he did. He'd read the letters.

And been stunned to learn of his mother's transgression. How she'd fled Hawaii as a young woman, away from their father, and fallen in love with another man.

And had given birth, upon her return, nine months later to twin boys—he and his brother, Nick.

A'Kela had passed on last year and, despite the lies, he, Nick and their father had loved her desperately. And missed her just as desperately.

It was obvious to Key that his father had known of their true parentage. Yet he'd never said a word. And he'd accepted Key and Nick as his own, never treating them as anything but his sons.

Key drew in a deep breath. Too many skeletons.

For all of that going on, *she* still remained the primary thought running roughshod inside his head.

"And that's saying a whole helluva lot, considering the type of day I've had," he muttered. "Damn." The curse was torn from his throat, grunted low.

Even as he blamed her, he knew she wasn't the one to blame. It seemed lately she'd been running 'round in his head so much, it was becoming the norm to fault her for everything from the constant stream of women tramping in and out to tour the Kealoha Ranch in an effort to see the Dynamic Duo, the cheesy nickname he and his brother seemed to be stuck with due to the reality show about the ranch, to the state of his constant hard-on.

He adjusted the front of his jeans absently and walked the stallion farther inside. No sooner had he'd walked inside than his steps halted and his gaze narrowed as it slid over the occupants of the massive stable.

He checked his irritation, barely, after seeing the small gathering of film crew that still lingered inside.

In the mood he was in, that was *just* what he needed to make his day complete.

"Damn," he growled as he walked his animal toward its stall.

After a long day helping his men brand the new shipment of cattle, including two new prize bulls, seeing his stable still teeming with film crew added more fuel to the fire already burning.

Yeah, that was just what the hell he needed.

Squashing the immediate need to tell them to get the hell off his property, Key gritted his jaw and recalled why he'd allowed the TV film crew on his family's property in the first place.

Family, ranch and preserving Hawaii. Those, and those alone, were his reasons for putting up with the intrusion into the daily lives of him and his family, ranch family included.

The attention from the show helped to bring awareness to the Aloha Keiki, the foundation his mother had started, which helped young, disadvantaged youth bring in much needed money to the poorer communities on the island. The money specifically was designated to help with agriculture, as well as scholarship opportunities for those who aspired to go to college. Through gardening and the community orchard his family had started years ago, which the children and volunteers tended to, the money it generated went to those families in need in the small town near the Kealoha Ranch.

At times the burden of responsibility and decisions he and Nick made on a daily basis, without their father's input, due to his recovery from the stroke he'd had after their mother's death, was overwhelming.

But it was a responsibility that he and his twin shouldered willingly.

Although when it came to the attention the show had given the ranch, his "player" of a brother was having less difficulty than Key because of the added attention from women.

He'd agreed to allow the television crew to come

in and film the lives of the men and women who worked the Kealoha Ranch to bring awareness, globally, to the impact of ranching in Hawaii as well attention for their mother's foundation. The desire he and his family had to preserve the environment while forging ahead in the new generation was a cause important to the Kealoha family.

It was what his father wanted, what he promised his wife he would always champion. A'Kela's recent passing had left a hole in their lives that could never be filled.

To that end, Key, Nick and their father, Alekanekelo Kealoha, had made sure to follow through with their promise.

And if allowing television cameras into their daily lives was what it took, Key was determined to go through with it. It was what his mother would have wanted. It had become the mantra for Key and his brother.

And now that his father was recovering from the massive stroke he'd suffered after the death of his wife, a woman he loved more than life, it was up to Keanu and Nick to make sure they honored their mother's last wish.

He drew in a deep sigh and turned narrowed eyes toward the gathering of *Borg*. The name brought a reluctant half smile to lift a corner of Key's wide mouth. His housekeeper, Mahi, had given the moniker to the collective crew.

At the age of sixty-five, Mahi was a self-proclaimed

junie of all things sci-fi with *Star Trek: The Next Generation* being one of his all-time favorites.

Key had to admit calling them the *Borg* was as good a definition as any, as they tended to present a collective nest type of thinking.

Which made him think of the one he referred to, privately in his own thoughts, as the Queen Borg....

Against his will his glance raked over the group, checking to see if the one who was the main source of both the state of his overall irritation, as well as his constant hard-on, was anywhere around.

He ignored the strum of disappointment when he didn't see her.

Although damn if he wouldn't know if she *were* there. Whenever the woman was within any distance of Key he could pick up her scent. He was no better than one of his prize stags in rut whenever she was within a fifty-yard radius.

He turned his attention back to his horse and began to remove the tack. Within moments, he slowly turned back in the direction of the film crew.

The Queen Borg...his inner voice mocked him. The name didn't come close to fitting the woman. She was fine, from head to damn toe, Key thought, frustration warring with his libido. He knew he'd given her the nickname, even if only in thought, in an effort to minimize the attraction he felt for the sexy, long-legged producer.

She strode toward the group, a small tablet in her

hand, her assistant close by. Key's attention went front and center on the woman who had occupied more space in his mind than he'd allowed a woman in a long, *long* time.

More than he had allowed any woman. The truth struck, deep and swift. He had never permitted any woman beyond family to get close to him.

As he watched her walk confidently toward the group of mostly men, he checked his rise of anger when several of them stood straighter, wide grins on their faces.

Although her assistant walked beside her, all eyes were on Sonia.

Not that he could blame them.

As soon as she approached the group, one of the men, the lighting technician he believed, clamped a hand on her shoulder. At this distance from the group Key couldn't see her clearly; however, there was something in her posture that made him wonder if she liked the familiar touch.

He felt the irrational anger rise again, and he swiftly took a step toward the group before he checked himself, his immediate response being the overwhelming need to *remove* the man's hand from her shoulder.

He frowned. What the hell was with him? It wasn't his business who she wanted to touch her, or not.

He ignored the mocking inner voice that called him a damn liar.

His hungry gaze traveled over her, from the top of

her shiny brown hair to the tips of her cowboy boots, a frown pulling his brows together.

She wore a white, sheer gauzy type of shirt that was opened to the waist, revealing a plain tank top underneath and soft jeans that, although they had several ripped spots scattered over them, appeared to be from actual wear and not manufactured. Even the cowboy boots she wore appeared to be authentic, not like the fashionable ones he'd noticed several of her crew wearing. Nine times out of ten he and his men laughed as, one by one, most of them stopped wearing them, as by the end of the day they were limping from pinched toes.

Even in her shoe choices, she was authentic and one of a kind, and admiration strummed through him despite his determination not to find anything more attractive about the woman.

He continued his perusal of her.

Nothing she wore screamed *sexy.* Nothing that *should* make him want to walk over, haul her up into his arms, throw her over his shoulder, take her to the nearest stall and see if she could make good on the promise of that hot little body of hers.

It wasn't the clothes getting him hot and bothered.

It was what her body *did* to the clothes that had his cock hardening to granite.

With breasts that made him think of two deliciously plump mounds of sweet, sinful chocolate ice cream, complete with succulent hard cherries on top, they were large but firm…with *just* enough jiggle to reduce a grown man to a teenage boy with one look.

Not to mention what the image of him lying between her legs as he sucked and tugged on those glorious breasts of hers did to him late at night when she tended to show up, nightly, in every dream he had.

Damn…Key drew in a breath. From experience he knew that within close proximity of each other, one look from him sent her nipples into hard peaks beneath his gaze. She was just as aware of him as he was of her.

He continued his long-distance appraisal. From his vantage point he caught the way her washed-out jeans molded and cupped her firm buttocks, appreciating the soft sway of her hips as she walked toward the group.

It made his palms itch, his imagination going into hyperdrive wondering if her ass would fit into both palms of his hands with the type of perfection he'd imagined in dreams he'd had of her, more erotic than any during his entire adolescence.

It didn't take much imagination on his part to imagine *just* how perfectly her cheeks would fit into his hands. No way around it. The woman had a glorious backside. Neither did it take a leap of imagination to envision how she would look naked, spread-eagle beneath him…or what he'd do to that soft, sweet ass of hers once he had both cheeks cupped in the palms of his hands as he stroked into her warmth.

And no one woman had ever accused Key of having a lack of imagination.

"Damn," he muttered, his cock painful in its hardness.

"Sir?"

One of his stable hands wrung his attention away from the sexy producer. He turned slowly, reluctantly away and glanced at the young man feeding one of his prize Thoroughbreds in the next stable.

Key shook his head as to clear it, yet found his attention torn between the stable boy and Sonia, whom he kept in his peripheral view.

When the lighting technician placed his beefy hand again on Sonia's shoulder and squeezed, Key gritted his teeth together, tightly, his short nails scoring grooves in his work-roughened palms as he gripped the horse's leather reins in both hands.

Before striding over to her, he turned back to the young stable boy. "Think you can take care of her for me, Hutch?" he asked, referring to his horse. His glance fell over the tall, gangly adolescent, this time giving the boy his full attention.

"Yes, sir!" The boy gave a swift pat on the rump of the horse he was currently attending and sprinted to Key's side, taking the leather reins from his hands.

Key felt a slow grin lift the corner of his mouth at the young man's reaction. Entrusting the boy with removing the horse's tack was no small thing as the horse in question was Key's prize Thoroughbred which he'd recently acquired in auction at an astronomical price.

"Take care of my girl, Hutch. She's special," he murmured, running a hand over the horse's back, yet his attention had already left both the horse and Hutch and was centered on Sonia again.

Key turned around, eyes narrowing, and he strode over to the small gathering, keeping his gaze locked and loaded on Sonia Brandon.

Chapter 2

Sonia didn't need to turn around to know who watched her.

She felt Keanu's intense, bright, blue-eyed gaze on her, searing her skin through the white gauzy blouse she wore over her tank top.

On cue, she felt her ridiculous nipples respond. She nonchalantly crossed her arms, hoping to hide her body's telling reaction.

As though it was the noonday sun, the heat from his stare scorched her skin, blazing hot and heavy against her neck. And the intensity brought the same reaction as the noonday sun; she was instantly hot and bothered.

Sonia reached a hand up and massaged her fingers over the back of her neck, hoping to relieve the suddenly bunched muscles. She forced herself to concentrate on her crew.

"I need a small group, including one of your assistants," she began, speaking to her film editor before turning to the others, "to follow the men heading out to the south pastures. The foreman has already okayed it, and recommended the crew get there by no later than 5:00 a.m." She held up a hand and waved it back and forth to negate the volley of protest she knew was coming her way. "I know they're just repairing fence, but it's all a part of ranch life. I don't want to miss out on an opportunity for some good promo like we did yesterday, Sheldon." She turned and pinned one of the location manager's assistants with a stare.

Although they'd been on site, filming for over two months steady, and would soon wrap up filming, Sonia knew from experience that there was no such thing as too much film.

Her location manager had recently gone on maternity leave and left her assistant in charge, believing, as everyone did, that the six-episode series was wrapping up and the crew disbanding. Although she was competent, as were all of the crew, the assistant manager was not as experienced as her boss and Sonia had been forced to do some quick training to get the young woman up to speed.

Sonia felt lucky to be working with such a talented and creative group on her series. Even though most of her crew were young by industry standards, they were excited to work with her, and they worked well together, just as eager as Sonia to see the show a success.

Sonia couldn't fault her location manager or her assistant, because in all honesty no one had had any idea the show would be such a megahit so quickly.

Sonia was proud of her crew, as she had been hands-on in the selection process once she'd signed on as producer.

After only a few airings, the show had gone nuclear. The hot new show, became the "it" show, garnering the type of ratings they'd only dreamed of in network television heaven. The response alone, after just the pilot episode, had been an indication to Sonia that the network would approve more episodes; however, before the last episode had been aired, she'd heard from the network execs that they wanted a full season. And today she'd been notified that the network wanted a second season, when the first hadn't even been completed.

To say the show was a success was putting it mildly. From the network executives to the chatter on social media, everyone knew they had a winner; the combination of ranch life and Hawaii was one their key audience seemed incredibly enthusiastic about.

Again, Sonia felt the heat from his stare on her back, making her body…tingle. She kept her attention focused on the meeting.

It wasn't just the beautiful location, exotic local

and unique features of a Hawaiian ranch that had been the reasons for the early success of the show.

It had been directly due to the appeal of the sexy twin bachelors, Keanu, "Key," and Nick Kealoha—that had been *the* major reason. And Sonia didn't need to see the show's research report to tell her that.

The twins had more sex appeal than any two men should be allowed, by state law, to have, and although they were identical twins, Keanu seemed to have a fraction…more appeal. At least for her.…

Whenever she was within visual distance of the man, all of her "Hollywood sophistication," as he'd once called it, went right out the window.

The man did it for her. Plain and simple.

Unfortunately, she did nothing for him. Well, outside of irritating the hell out of the man. She sighed.

Keanu seemed to have a permanent scowl on his face whenever she was around him. But none of that mattered, anyway. It was probably a good thing she did nothing for him in the way of attraction, because it couldn't go anywhere.

Not that she could or had let Keanu know exactly how attracted she was to him. She was the producer on the show, not one of the hundreds of groupies the ranch seemed to have, women who came by the site just to get a glimpse of Hawaii's new Dynamic Duo, the cheesy but—Lord only knows—accurate name the sexy twin ranch owners had been dubbed by the media.

"The show is doing great, better than expected.

The ratings are continuing to top the number-one spot," Sonia stated, forcing thoughts of Keanu from her mind and focusing on her staff. "And we've been renewed for a second season!" She waited for the exclamations of excitement to calm. She had just been given the news, and although she wasn't all that sure that they'd be able to convince the Kealohas, in particular Keanu Kealoha, to allow them to continue, she kept that part to herself.

She smiled at her staff, knowing pride was in her voice. But she had invested a lot in the show. Once she had agreed to produce it, she'd made sure that every aspect of the show was given attention it deserved.

She knew that Keanu and his family had given permission initially to bring awareness of the impact of ranching on the environment to not only Hawaii but also the world. It wasn't for the money, as they were one of the most profitable ranches in Hawaii. Neither was it for attention, even though the ranch now had tours for tourists, mostly women coming out to see the sexy twins of Kealoha Ranch.

They had done it for a much more noble reason. Although she didn't fully understand the whys of his agreement, she hadn't looked a gift horse in the mouth after he'd finally agreed.

Her only hope was that Keanu would continue to tolerate them on his ranch, as more and more she got the impression the sexy cowboy was less than pleased with their presence.

"Is the direction for the show going to change?" Briana, her director of photography, drawled the question.

"That's a good question. So far the objective remains the same—why tamper with what works? As for a second season and the direction, we're going to keep going in the same vein. Show all aspects of ranch life. We can worry later about editing out what doesn't work."

"Now Ms. Sonia, you can not deny that a big part of what is making the show a hit is Mr. Fine and his equally gorgeous brother...Mr. Finer," the woman drawled, her Southern accent and way she drew out the word *fine* making Sonia laugh despite herself.

Briana was from Tennessee, and her drawling manner of speech, up-front manner and dry wit, coupled with the magic she brought to the angle of her camera had been the reasons Sonia had hired her to lead the camera department.

"I say we take it up a notch! I can see it now," she began, warming up to her theatrics. She closed her eyes and placed her hands in front of her face, mimicking a camera as she spoke. "Sweat dripping from their naked chests, the amber glow of the setting sun behind them as the twins come home from a long, *hard* day, wrangling—" she paused dramatically "—cattle."

Everyone laughed at her antics, including Sonia. Besides the magic she brought to her camera work, drama was most definitely Briana's middle name.

But that same drama, when channeled, was what also had brought the young woman awards in her field.

"Of course I am fully aware of the…impact…of the twins on the show," Sonia conceded, and held up a hand admitting defeat once the laughter died. "I just don't want to miss out on good footage. That is what makes the show work. All aspects. Fine is wonderful, it works," she said, and ignored the snicker of laughter from her female-dominated crew. "But if we don't capture the heart of the ranching life, it's all just fluff," she replied, sobering. "And not only do I not produce fluff, I don't want to do the ranch a disservice." She finished and saw heads nodding in agreement.

"We won't miss good footage again, Sonia. I'll make sure of it!" her assistant replied, bobbing her head up and down as she stood beside Sonia. "In fact, I'll be out on location in the morning with them to make sure of it," she replied.

"Great, Patricia, I'm sure Bri would appreciate anything you can do to help her accomplish that objective," Sonia carefully replied. "Now let's quickly finish the schedule."

Again Sonia unconsciously rubbed at the back of her neck as her glance fell over the schedule, her fingers on the screen of her iPad as she flipped through the digital pages on-screen as the crew gathered their own notes, comparing them with the others.

"Tired, boss?"

She glanced away from the small screen of her iPad as she turned to Patricia, frowning.

"Saw you rubbing your neck. It's been a long day…" Patricia murmured, sympathy in her tone.

Sonia brought her hand down immediately. It wasn't the long day that made her rub her neck. It was *him*.

She didn't have to turn around to know who was in the large stable, along with her staff and the young stable boys who worked the Kealoha.

She refused to give him even that much power over her.

She brought a purposeful smile to her face. "Yes, it's been a long day, but I'm fine, Tricia. But thanks," she tacked on, seeing the crestfallen look on the older woman's face.

She was always careful with her assistant's feelings, even when the woman made some crazy faux pas or screwed up a location site, Sonia covered for her, something that was becoming harder and harder to do, each day.

In a lot of ways, she felt empathy for the older woman. It wasn't easy, the business they were in. So much competition to not only get to the top of their field but stay there, as well.

At one point in her career, Patricia had been on her way to the top; however, bad choices, both career and personal—in the way of drinking—had drastically changed her career path. Paranoid, due to the alcohol, Tricia began to blame those who worked for her for sloppy mistakes. Mistakes that were actually hers, and hers alone.

It didn't take long for her to gain a reputation as not only an alcoholic but one who mistreated her staff, blaming them for her mistakes.

She'd eventually gotten help for the drinking. But it had come too little, too late.

Despite all of that, Sonia felt a deep sense of loyalty to her once mentor and felt as though she owed Patricia.

As a young woman, Sonia had interned with Patricia Haynes, who at the time had been affiliated with both a major network as well as public television network. As the producer of several shows on a local public television, Patricia had wielded a certain amount of power. The two women had clicked, with Patricia sharing valuable information with Sonia, willing and eager to help Sonia in any way she could as she learned the ins and outs of producing a television show. She'd told Sonia she reminded her of herself at her age.

This had all happened before the downhill sprawl in her career.

When Sonia's career had grown exponentially, and she'd eventually been offered her first show to produce with a major cable network, she'd immediately thought of Patricia and called her mentor to ask if she'd be interested in working with her.

Initially, Sonia had been concerned that Patricia would be offended, as she would serve as Sonia's assistant, but was relieved when the woman had eagerly taken her up on the offer, and they'd been working together every since.

That wasn't the only reason for her hesitancy.

Added to all of that, Patricia had originally been set to produce the show.

However, the show hadn't ever really gotten off the ground. The ideas that Patricia had come up with to showcase the ranch had fallen flat on the executives. After languishing for two years, no real work had been done to develop the story line, until Sonia was approached by Marty Shop and Sheldon Harris and the deal had been renegotiated. Sonia was becoming well-known in the industry and the two executives had felt that under her directorship, the show would sparkle. Hesitantly, she'd agreed to view the footage they'd already shot.

And she'd been hooked. But she wouldn't consider doing it without asking Patricia to come on board. She felt she owed the woman at least that much.

Although at times Patricia made a caustic comment and Sonia felt as though Patricia was jealous of her success, she'd immediately feel awful for thinking that way. The woman had always been her biggest champion, and had it not been for the older woman, she wouldn't have gotten her early break into the business.

"So, that's it for the day. Why don't you pack up and get some rest. Tomorrow is going to be an early one, and with the holiday coming up, let's get as much work in as we can. No telling how crazy it's going to be in a few weeks!"

"Oh, no…don't remind me!" Patricia piped up. With the Fourth of July around the corner, coupled with an expected increase in holiday tourism, the Kealoha Ranch, as well as the crew, were gearing up for an avalanche of spectators.

"Which reminds me, I need to go to the trailer and download the production schedule from corporate." Sonia barely refrained from groaning. It had been a long day and she was beyond tired.

She reached a hand up and again began to massage her tired neck muscles. Not to mention the fact that Key was eyeing her down. The longer she'd stood speaking with the crew and Patricia, the more heated his stare had become. She hadn't even had to turn his way to know that.

She felt that familiar fissure of sharp awareness curl through her stomach, winding its way throughout her body, and the resulting spike of goose bumps to sprinkle over her skin.

"I'll take care of that, boss, it's been quite a day. Me and the guys are headed that way on the way back to the hotel." A big, beefy hand touched Sonia's back and she barely refrained from wincing. "In fact, before heading to the hotel, we're going to hit the Wave for a few drinks," he began, mentioning one of the nightclubs not far from the hotel where they were staying. He stopped and smiled down at her, the dimple in one of his chubby cheeks flashing as he extended the invitation. "You're welcome to join us."

"Thanks, Walt," she replied, smiling up at the large man. "Maybe some other time. I've got some work to do in my room before I hit the bed."

"Well, anytime you change your mind, let me— us—know."

She saw the disappointed look enter his dark eyes before he nodded his head and turned with the others to leave.

She nodded and smiled before she dismissed her crew, after giving final instructions for the next day's filming.

"It will be a light day tomorrow, everyone. I don't expect us to go past noon, and after that, the next few days are yours!" Her response elicited the expected pleased reaction from her staff, bringing a genuine grin to lift the corners of her lips.

She watched the group leave and drew in a deep breath. She knew who she now had to face.

"Looks like it's time to saddle up," Tricia murmured, and Sonia bit back a groan in reply.

She didn't have to turn around to know whom Patricia was talking about. And her assistant's reference to saddling up didn't help *at all*....

Sonia sighed and closed her eyes briefly. She remembered the way Keanu had spoken the heart-felt words to her over the phone after he'd finally agreed to do the show and allow her and her crew on his land.

"The new generation, our generation…we all need to come together and work on the environment to survive. Not just in Hawaii but all over the world. If the Kealoha Ranch can help in any way…we're ready to saddle up, ma'am." His deep baritone had washed over her like a hot shower.

As the producer of several hit shows, when she'd been approached about filming a reality show, her first response had been a hearty "hell no!" Not a fan of reality TV in general, she'd always found herself cringing whenever she'd watched it. Even though she had secretly watched a couple, she would never consider producing one.

After viewing the footage the network had provided, her thoughts had changed. They had sent a small film crew over to the island to secretly take film footage of the Kealoha Ranch, located on the beautiful Hana, Big Island, Hawaii, and after viewing, despite herself, Sonia had been intrigued with the idea of a Hawaiian ranch, something she hadn't ever associated with Hawaii.

Within days she'd booked a flight.

The footage hadn't done the island justice. After her first night staying at one of the luxury resorts, she'd risen early, unable to stay in bed. Coffee in hand, she'd walked over to the large window and stood staring out in awe, taking in the breathtaking view.

The scene could have been plucked from a blockbuster movie, it was so surreally beautiful.

The beautiful eucalyptus and ohia trees, lolling hills in the distance and the vividly blue wide-open Pacific all made for a magnificent backdrop to the incredible scene.

Sonia had then taken a ride out to the Kealoha Ranch and her fate had been sealed. The unique blend of emerald-blue water, tranquil skies and ranching assured her the project would be a winner.

The ranch and island had captured her imagination and Sonia had eagerly accepted the gig.

But it had taken a lot more than a simple phone call to convince the reclusive rancher to agree. Originally A'Kela Kealoha had agreed to do the show; however, there were production challenges and the show went on hold.

The producers had decided to try again and had contacted Alekanekelo Kealoha, only to learn of the elder Kealoha's illness and the family's need for privacy after the death of his wife. Disappointed, Sonia and the others had begun to believe the show wouldn't be able to be produced.

When they learned there were two other men, the twin sons of Alek Kealoha, Keanu and Nick Kealoha, who were equal partners, they'd approached them in a final effort. With Nick they'd been elated when he'd agreed…only to laughingly tell them it was his "big" brother they now had to convince. His identical twin, who was older than Nick by a full five minutes.

And that had been the beginning of a six-month

courtship between Sonia and Keanu, via email, Messenger and iChat.

When she'd learned of his involvement with a local volunteer group that sought to bring awareness about preserving Hawaii's natural habitat, as well as the foundation his mother had started to help those in need, she'd quickly devised a new angle and brought the proposal to his attention.

When the new angle seemed to appeal to him, she'd barely held her excitement in check when Pat had come into her office, nearly bursting with the news that the fuddy-duddy, as she'd dubbed him, was on line one, waiting for her.

Sonia had taken a deep breath, closed her eyes and prayed to the Almighty for patience before putting a smile on her face and answering the phone. She found that when she smiled while dealing with irritating, overbearing men who thought they knew it all, it helped center her, even if they couldn't see her fake smile.

"This is Sonia Brandon, may I help you?" she'd asked, infusing more than a little bit of confidence into her voice. Another thing she did while dealing with the aforementioned group.

"The new generation, our generation...we all need to come together and work on the environment to survive. Not just in Hawaii but all over the world. If the Kealoha Ranch can help in any way...we're ready to saddle up, ma'am."

With those words, he'd gotten under her skin.

Those words issued in that deep, sexy-as-sin velvet voice…

She'd blown out a long breath as soon as she'd severed the connection, with a deal tentatively reached.

God…she hadn't even had to meet the man for him to get her hot and bothered.

Or maybe it had been too dang long since she'd had a man.

Whatever it was, he'd caught her attention from that moment on…and it had only gotten worse.

After a round-table discussion with key players from the network, the executive producer and Sonia, they'd decided to try once more and had been surprised when he'd agreed. And as soon as they'd all met the reclusive rancher, Patricia had soon stopped calling the handsome rancher "fuddy-duddy."

"Ms. Brandon…a word." The sinfully deep voice sent her heart skipping, brought her back to the present with a rush.

"Patricia, why don't you—" Sonia stopped and cleared her throat from the frog lodged firmly in the back. She kept her cool, her smile firmly in place. "Why don't you take the rest of the evening off. We're done here." She ignored the spark in her assistant's eyes as she ran them back and forth between Sonia and the man behind her.

Although Patricia never said anything, Sonia knew the woman suspected Sonia was attracted to the rancher. However, she'd prudently refrained from asking, instinctively knowing that although they were close it would be crossing the line.

"Are you sure? I could—"

"Patricia…yes. Please," she interrupted, still trying to hold it together. Before Patricia could leave, Sonia remembered that she'd forgotten to advise the crew about the change in meeting time. "Patricia, could you let the staff know that I'd like to meet with them tomorrow, at lunchtime?" Sonia hoped that giving Patricia the right to relay information to the staff would mollify her and remove the suddenly wooden expression from her assistant's face. Normally, she wasn't so abrupt with Patricia, but lately…well, chalk it up to overactive hormones and Keanu Kealoha, she thought, mentally drawing in a deep breath.

"Right away, boss," Patricia replied, her voice slightly cooled.

"I'm sorry. I didn't mean to offend," she began, placing a hand on her assistant's arm.

Although she was sincerely sorry if she had offended Patricia, at the moment, her assistant's feelings were not primary in her thoughts.

"Don't worry about it, Sonia. I understand," Patricia replied, her expression lightening.

"Ms. Brandon." The deep baritone had a distinctly irked quality, reminding her that Keanu Kealoha wasn't a man accustomed to having to wait on *anyone*.

She suppressed a ridiculous shiver. His voice warned Sonia that she and the irritating man attached to the sexy, drop-your-panties voice were going to have yet another…*uncomfortable* encounter. The thought brought a shiver, again, to run down her spine.

She straightened her back, mentally reminding herself that, no, she was most definitely *not* looking forward to any type of encounter with him. Unless it was business. Strictly business.

She ignored the self-mocking inner laugh.

She drew in a breath, subtly tugging down the hem of her casual tank top back inside the waistband of her jeans, realizing that it had ridden up, exposing her stomach. She had no intention of him even *thinking* she was doing anything to get his…attention.

It was strictly business with Keanu Kealoha, she reminded herself, again.

Sonia drew in a breath. Despite her every intention of not letting him know *just* how much he affected her she knew he'd guess in a heartbeat if she didn't get it together. Placing a faux look of confidence and casual smile on her face, she turned to face him.

But damn…really? Did he have to be *so* ridiculously fine?

Sonia mentally groaned, her helpless gaze raking over his tall, muscular body.

"I think it's long overdue that you and I got to know each other, Ms. Brandon."

It wasn't just what he said that made her legs threaten to buckle, although that alone caused her heart to hiccup with the implication of his words. More than that, it was the way he said it that caused the queasiness to settle in her gut, the kind of queasy feeling a woman got when a man turned her on so bad she didn't know the last time she'd felt so hot and bothered. It was the *way* he said it, and the way his bright eyes raked her over, head to toe, that made her feel naked, exposed.

And wanted.

Dear God…

Suddenly all kinds of forbidden, delicious images came to mind.

Images of how…*what,* she could do to convince him to allow the series to continue. A slow, warm heat flushed her entire body at the thought, an unknown grin creasing the edges of her full lips upward.

She turned to face him.

Chapter 3

Was he the cause for the sexy little grin on her face? Key wondered, feeling a jolt in the region of his heart at the glint in Sonia's dark brown eyes, and the mischievous-looking smile on her full lips. Everything about her appealed to him on levels he never knew existed.

As she stood before him, doe-eyed and staring at him with a sexy glint, it was all he could do not to fulfill every one of the erotic dreams he'd had of her over the past few months. Hell, the dreams, although hot as any of the active volcanoes around the island, would look like a cartoon compared to what he wanted to do to her.

But he knew better than to make good on those dreams. She would be gone soon, leaving him, the ranch and the island, like all the rest. And that smile of hers was one he shouldn't trust, he knew that, no matter how damn sexy it, or she, was.

"So glad you could make time to speak to me, Ms. Brandon," he began, and immediately saw her reaction to his words. The smile dipped and waned before she forced it to remain. But it wasn't the same. Although brighter, it was less authentic. She lifted her chin just a fraction higher, her back stiffening. For a moment, Key wished he could retract his words.

Although she was of average height, the top of her head reached him midchest and, in order for her to make eye contact with him, she had to take a step back as well as lift her chin. The fact that he was trying to convince himself that that was the reason for her stepping back from him, he ignored.

"Such a hard-ass," she mumbled, but he caught the words.

"Excuse me?" Key asked, shock warring with genuine humor.

Her eyes flew to his and she covered her mouth, her eyes wide. "You, uh, heard that?" she asked.

"Yeah. But it's okay. I've been called worse," he replied, shrugging a shoulder.

"I'll bet you have," she returned, and he caught the red flush stain her creamy brown cheeks.

"Oh, God, I'm sorry, I didn't mean—"

"It's okay. Like I said, I've been called much, much worse," he replied, cutting into her apology.

When she grinned again, it threw him off guard

and he felt himself responding to her gamine expression.

She had a smile on her face that reminded him of Nick. Although he and Nick were identical on the outside, when it came to women they were as different as night and day, with Nick playing the role of playboy rancher to the hilt. Her smile was about as sincere as his twin's avowals of devotion to any one of his girlfriends.

In other words, bogus.

Even as her snappy answers and overall sassy attitude aggravated him, Key couldn't deny the effect her curvy body and cute ass had on him. His eyes fell to her full lips. The bottom curve poked out just a hint, giving her a natural pouty expression, one that played hell on his libido, wondering what it would taste like.

He'd thought about it, tasting that full, luscious lip of hers, drawing it into his mouth to suckle and kiss.

Each time he did, he remembered that she was only in his life for a while. She, like all the rest, would be gone once her season was over.

He'd do well to remember that. It was only physical, his reaction to her. Once she and her crew had left the island, his life and his libido would return to normal.

He drew in a breath, remembering what he had recently discovered.

Did she have information about what he'd discovered somehow? Had she or someone in her camp found out that he and Nick were the sons of Jede-diah Clint Wilde, whose adoptive sons were the legal owners of the Wilde Ranch, one of the most prof-itable family-owned-and-operated ranches in the United States? Was that the reason she'd approached his brother about extending the season?

The idea had plagued him since he and his brother had spoken days ago and Nick had casually informed him about the request to continue the show. Even before he could continue, Key had already begun shaking his head.

"Not only no, but hell no," he'd said, his jaw tight-ening. "Look, you know the only reason we agreed to do this was to honor Mom's last request. Well, we've done that. We've helped raise awareness and with that Mom's foundation for the preservation of Hawaii has tripled in donations. As for the rest…the attention from the show, attention I sure as hell am damn sick of—"

"Well, I'm not," his brother had cut in. His arms were crossed as he leaned against the kitchen table, one big booted foot crossed over the other, a half grin on his face as he observed his brother's rising anger, no doubt enjoying the hell out it while calmly munching on an apple.

"It is done. Finished. With the foundation having a higher profile, donations will continue. I've been the *good son*," he'd said, turning away from Nick.

He knew that his brother was in tune with him, more than anyone. And keeping his thoughts and emotions hidden from Nick for too long was damn hard to do.

But Key had to do exactly that, at least until he figured out how...*when* he'd share what he'd learned about who they were with his brother.

The role his father had had in the deception was not far from his mind, either. Hell, he didn't have a clue how he'd approach Alek Kealoha, the only man he or his brother had ever called Father.

For now, regarding their parents' dishonesty, he would hold his tongue, as well as his emotions, firmly in check.

He'd turned to face Nick.

"Look, Kaikaina," he'd begun, not realizing that in his distress he'd called his brother by his Hawaiian nickname. "The only reason I agreed to this invasion of our home in the first place was because of Mom and the foundation. Now that we've accomplished that goal, there's no way in hell I'm going to agree to a second season. One was pushing it. But it was for Mom, so..." He shrugged and paused, ran a hand through his hair and allowed the sentence to dangle.

Even through his anger, his feelings of betrayal, he loved his mother, as did his brother. And, even knowing what he now did, he would have still allowed the crews to film because the foundation had meant everything to her.

"This was for Mom, yeah, man, I get that. Dad and I agreed with you, remember? I'm not the bad guy here."

"Hell, Nick, I never said or thought you were. You're my brother. You're family. And family comes first," he'd said.

There'd been a pause, as both men grew serious.

"Yeah, I get that. I also get that you don't want them here—"

"But you and Dad do. So for that reason, I'm cool with it, bro."

There was another small silence before Nick broke in, his voice gruff. "Mom would have wanted it. I know you could have persuaded Dad that you were against it. But I think it's a good idea, Key."

"Hell. I guess," Key had replied as he'd glanced away from his brother. When Nick shoved away from the doorway and clapped his brother on the back he turned back to face him.

"Dad, yes…but you know damn well a part of the reason you want this is for the women. Damn player," Key said, a small grin on his face.

"Well, what can I say, big brother…gotta give 'em what they want," he said, and flexed large biceps.

"Man…whatever," Key responded before he shoved his brother away, and both men laughed.

"And if some high-society producer thinks she can go around me and get the answer she wants, she has another damn think coming. Discussion over," he'd replied firmly, humor evaporating as the image of Sonia came back to his mind, his thoughts.

His jaws tightened.

"Somebody's got his shorts in a knot over said

high-society producer, I see," had been his twin's laughing retort.

To which he'd given him the anticipated single-finger salute answer. Looking at his brother was like looking at a mirror image of himself. So, when his brother lifted one brow and laughed, Key found himself hoping he didn't look like a damn laughing hyena, as well.

Key had left the room, ignoring Nick's taunting laugh.

Although they were identical twins, the two men played women very differently. Yet for all of their differences, Nick knew him, just as Key knew Nick, better than anyone else.

Key knew that Nick was aware that Sonia Brandon had gotten under his skin, but he didn't give a damn. He would take pleasure in telling her no and had been waiting for nearly a week to do just that.

He stared down at her, rubbing the back of his neck.

That was before he'd discovered who and where… he and his brother were linked to. And with that, he wondered if Sonia Brandon knew about the big-ass skeletons in his closet, skeletons he was determined to keep exactly where they belonged, deep in the closet.

And if they didn't know, Key was determined that the sexy producer and her staff would not find out. He knew if they did, they would do everything to exploit his family. His family had been through enough with the death of his mother and his father's massive stroke soon after…life had been rocky. They were all just recovering from the loss, moving on and living, and he was damned if he'd allow anyone to come in and destroy that.

The fact that he himself had just learned about the Wildes, in particular his and Nick's birthright, gave Key some confidence that he was the only one outside of his father who knew. But no mistake about it, it was a rocky confidence.

Because, although he dismissed the possibility that Sonia knew, he was going to cover all of his bases. He would be the one to figure out not only how to tell his brother, but if and when they would make contact with the Wildes. And if that happened, something so private damn well wouldn't be broadcast before millions of people.

He was determined she or anyone in her crew would not discover his and Nick's connection to the Wildes. To that end, he kept in mind there was an outside chance that particular egg was already out of the basket.

After wrestling with the decision, and not knowing for sure in the end, Key relied on one of his father's favorite sayings: keep your friends close and your enemies closer. Not that she was exactly his enemy, but Key wasn't trustful of the industry to which she belonged.

So if he had to make a deal with the devil…he glanced down at the beautiful woman who had been playing around in his mind from the moment they met. In all truth, from the moment he'd heard her husky, low, sexy voice, something about her had… intrigued him.

He would play her for a little longer. Until he found out exactly what, if anything, she knew about the skeletons in his family closet.

To that end, he knew he'd have to promise her something—himself.

"I'd like to make a proposition, Ms. Brandon," he said, keeping his face neutral. He carefully examined her features, searching for any signs that would clue him in to what she was up to, let him know if she had inside knowledge of his family.

"And what would that be, Mr. Kealoha?" Sonia asked, her dark brown, clear gaze locked with his, her face devoid of any telling emotions, anything to alert him that she was hiding something.

The woman was good.

She definitely knew how to play her cards close, Key thought in admiration. She had a poker face that would give the reigning poker champ a run for his money. But her voice…the natural husky timbre in her voice sounded nearly breathless. It was her weakness. He knew she had no idea that her voice was so telling, as he'd witnessed.

She'd had his ranch workers eating out of the palm of her hand from the first moment she spoke to them. Just as he had, they'd sat up straight, their attention closely given to the small woman with the sexy voice.

Not that it had only been her voice that the men had reacted to.

Uncontrollably his glance fell to the crest of her breasts. Each inhalation and exhalation he watched with a focused, helpless stare, as though he was caught by some invisible traction and couldn't look away.

"Ahem...I'm waiting," she said, and coughed.

Damn.

Embarrassed that he'd been gawking at her tits like some overgrown adolescent, the crazy spell was broken and his glance met hers.

One delicate brow was lifted, her lips pursed as though she was pissed to the max. Which only served to make his cock even harder. She was so damn sexy, even mad she turned him on.

If possible, Key felt even more like the overgrown kid she reduced him to whenever he was in her presence.

He tightened his jaw and mentally ordered his cock to *stand down* and act like the grown man it was attached to.

"I would like to propose that you stay close to me. I'm extending an invitation for you to be my 'right hand' so to speak," he began, lowering his voice, hoping to seduce her into feeling...comfortable around him.

If she was for him, she couldn't be against him.

"Allow me to show you why I agreed to the show, initially. Allow me to demonstrate to you why I love this ranch." He turned, extending his arm out to en-compass the ranch. "Why I love this land."

"And in exchange for that…?" she asked, allow-ing the sentence to dangle.

Key held his grin of satisfaction at bay. He could tell that he'd gotten her attention.

Good.

Her dark brown eyes lit with interest, and her small pink tongue came out to swipe across her full bottom lip. Just like her voice, the small action was a giveaway for her. One he was sure she hadn't real-ized she did whenever she was…intrigued.

His gaze zeroed in on the sexy movement. Damn, just when he was getting control of the situation she got him.

His cock thumped against the zipper on his jeans in direct response to her nipples, which had, as though on cue and defying the confines of her bra, proudly pressed against the tank top she wore. As though reaching for him.

Before he realized his own intent, he took a step forward. Taking her hand in his, he brought it up, forcing her into closer contact with him.

"I give you me. I will be more involved in the show, make more of an appearance on the show," he began, and held up a hand when he saw a light enter her beautiful dark eyes. "To a degree," he cautioned. "I want the audience to come to love the land as we do. For them to understand why we feel the way we do, they have to believe it. You have to believe it. Do you believe, Ms. Brandon?" he asked, tilting her chin forward.

She slowly nodded, her gaze focused on him. He had her right where he wanted her to be.

"And you'll sign on for a second season, Keanu?" she asked, her gaze direct.

The way she said his name again forced a reaction from his body, one he was struggling to keep in control.

Although he wasn't ready to make that final concession, he knew he had to give her something. He nodded.

"I think it will make for a good show. And it's all about the show, right, Ms. Brandon?" he asked, avoiding a direct answer. When her gaze narrowed, the slightest bit, he knew she'd caught the way he'd sidetracked answering.

He'd have to be careful around her.

Beauty, killer body and a sharp mind…it all added up to trouble.

Chapter 4

What in the world did he want her to make of *that?*

Sonia gnawed on her bottom rip, her eyes fixed on Keanu, her gaze running over his tall lanky form as he leaned negligently against the railing.

He'd dropped her hand before it had even registered that he'd held it and turned, his face now in profile.

Even as he was making his demands, or odd requests, annoying her to the nth degree, Sonia couldn't help admiring the man he was. She knew that he was only looking after his family, but each time he said some of the things he did to her, it set her teeth on *edge*. It wasn't always what he said, but the way he said it.

She refused to admit it, but deep inside his obvious mistrust of her…hurt.

There was something in his eyes that told her the request went beyond a need for her to understand his love for the land. She had always known he loved his home, his birthright. She'd also known from day one that he simply tolerated her presence, as well as the crew on his land, for the sake of his mother's foundation. So…what else was it? What had changed his mind? she wondered.

After approaching his brother about the possibility of a second season, she'd been surprised when he'd shot her down before the request had fully escaped her mouth.

"Well, as much as I'd like to oblige you, and the show, I'm going to have to say you stand as good as chance as a monkey's balls in hell of that getting past my brother," he'd said, and despite herself, she'd laughed.

"Uh, okay. Not really sure what that means," she said, shrugging. "But can I ask why?" she'd said, going for broke. She knew that if she couldn't at least get Nick to be on her team, there was slim to no chance of his more obstinate brother agreeing to the second season.

Although she didn't know if they had a close relationship, Key and his brother were as identical as two people could be. Both were tall—at a guess she'd place them around six foot three or four. Both had the same startling blue eyes and slightly olive complexion, high cheekbones, aquiline nose and chiseled chin.

Both men even sported the same slight bump in the centers of their noses. She'd thought when she'd met Nick, that it had been acquired by way of sports; however, she'd wondered if that were the case after she'd met Keanu and seen that both men shared the exact same imperfection, in the exact same spot.

She knew they were what people referred to as mirror twins, after hearing one of the interns mention it, but to have injuries in the same spot seemed a bit odd to her.

Both had thick, jet-black hair, given to curling on the ends, if left too long. But, as much as they looked alike, Sonia knew the brothers apart. For her it had been no question who was who.

Keanu...did it for her. She stopped trying to pretend that he didn't affect her, long ago. She simply had learned to deal with it, grateful that no one else knew how badly she had it for the sexy rancher.

Well, that was everyone except her assistant.

When Sonia had easily identified them, at first the staff had been surprised, wondering how she could when no one else could. She'd shrugged it off, inwardly embarrassed. She hoped her secret remained, that the reason she could differentiate between the two men was because she was so attracted to Keanu.

She'd caught her assistant observing her, keenly, as she'd laughed it off. But then she found out Patricia wasn't the only one. Once Nick learned that she could tell him and his brother apart, after hearing her crew laughing about it, she'd caught him on more than one occasion watching her, as well, particularly if his brother was anywhere around.

Sonia felt unnerved by Nick's stare. Not that it was overtly sexual; in fact, it was the opposite. She would have preferred the playboy flirting a lot better, she thought. That one she could handle. From the time she'd hit adolescence, she'd been dealing with men hitting on her. Besides, Sonia wondered about the over-the-top playboy role he played—how much was real and how much was simply for show.

He flirted and played with every woman under the age of eighty and seemed to have every one of them eating out of his hand. Yet for all of his flirting, she'd never seen Nick take any one of the many, many offers she'd seen thrown his way, usually from those women who visited the ranch hoping to meet the sexy Dynamic Duo.

But as much as she believed it was a role he played, he and his brother couldn't have been more different. Whereas Nick flirted with the women, from the crew to those who hung outside the ranch gates hoping for a peep inside, Keanu avoided them all like the plague. Especially Sonia.

Keanu. She sighed. Sonia knew he was the reason for his brother's reaction.

She felt like mentally screaming. Keanu turned her on, infuriated her and confused her all in equal amounts.

She covertly ran a gaze over him as he casually leaned back against the wrought-iron gate and crossed his big arms over his chest, staring out at the waning sunset. Although his face was away from hers, Sonia knew he was waiting for her reaction.

She got the feeling that her calm demeanor unnerved him, just as the standoffish, mistrustful vibe she'd gotten from him from day one did to her. But, again, she refused to let him know just how much he did affect her.

She wasn't sure when it had happened as they'd been speaking, but during the course of the conversation they'd left the stable and were now standing near one of the small corrals, alone, the dying rays of the sun fading behind the majestic mountains beyond the sea.

She drew in a breath and kept her glance on him. Head to toe, he was the epitome of sexy cowboy. Confidence poured from the man, from the way he spoke to his men to the way he handled the ranch.

From the first moment of filming, Sonia had known they had something special on their hands. Both Keanu and Nick, along with their father, were as authentic as they could have hoped for.

Not in the least excited about the crew, neither were they intimidated; in fact, if anything, it had been the crew that had initially been intimidated by the men. Although Nick was definitely a playboy, charm and ooze pouring from every fine inch of him, he worked his land just as hard as his brother and their men. Usually when filming reality shows the effort to keep the "real" in reality had been a dicey point, and was one of the reasons she'd always found them distasteful. And cheesy. The cheesy part was *the worst,* for Sonia.

It went down one of two ways. Either the ones being filmed were hyperaware of the camera and were stiff and unnatural, or they were over-the-top wannabe TV stars. Neither one had work for Sonia, so she'd always stuck with scripted shows. But, when the filming of the ranch had started, surprisingly the cowboys who worked the ranch had, after initial hesitancy, continued on with the job at hand, completely ignoring the crew.

Although most of the ranch hands were seasoned cowboys, there were also younger men, and they too had gone on to work as though the cameras weren't around. She knew the reason for that was the leadership. After meeting Nick, she'd realized that although he played the part of playboy to the hilt, behind the easy smile lay a completely different man, one who took his ranch seriously. After meeting Keanu, the complete puzzle had come together.

And when she'd first laid eyes on him…Sonia had known on that level of feminine intuition located deep, deep inside of every woman that she was in trouble.

"Who the hell is making all of this damn noise, scaring the crap out of my new horse?" The deep, booming baritone's ringing question stopped everyone, Sonia included, dead in their tracks as they'd gathered inside the massive stable to go over the production schedule.

It had been the first day of filming and everyone, including Sonia, was hyped and excited. She had arrived before both the crew and Patricia to get a feel for the direction she wanted to go. It wasn't that she wasn't prepared; in fact, whenever she approached any job, she was usually over prepared. This time was different for her.

Doing a reality series was different—something that, although it was supposed to be reality, she knew, like everyone else who watched it, that the shows were as scripted as any given Hollywood sitcom. But she'd been determined that hers would be as unique as the Kealoha Ranch was itself. After spending time with the ranch hands, time the owners had allowed, without interference, she'd known her ideal of being natural and real was the best way to go.

And after meeting Keanu, she'd known her decision was sound. One look at the tall, breathtakingly handsome cowboy had literally taken her breath away.

Although she'd not managed, during the week she was at the Kealoha Ranch before the crew, to see Keanu, as he'd been away the first days of her arrival, she'd spoken with and met his brother and identical twin, Nick, and had already been impressed with his twin's good looks and natural charm. Identical in every way on the outside, both men possessed the type of looks that she knew a camera would eat up.

When her director of photography had openly stared at Keanu, her camera dangling at her side, whispering "hot damn," she'd turned to face the man attached to the booming voice.

And from that moment on, she'd been hooked.

Her glance fell to him now as he silently stood next to her.

She couldn't really tell anyone the whys of it. Yes, he was one of the most gorgeous men she'd ever laid eyes on, but it was more than that.

Normally he wore the typical cowboy hat worn by most on the cowboys, low on his head, covering his hair. But of course, on Keanu it was anything but typical. The way the hat sat low, obscuring most of his face, with only the lower half showing sent goose bumps over her flesh when she'd catch him eyeballing her whenever he was near.

When she'd once seen him take it off and wipe a handkerchief across his forehead, cleaning off the sweat, she had felt her heart nearly pound out of her chest.

After removing the hat, his mop of shiny black strands were mussed over his head, looking as though he had just gotten out of bed. Immediately the image came to mind of a woman's hands being the one that caused the muss.

And, of course, those hands doing the mussing were hers.

He reached up to remove the hat, allowing it to dangle in his big hands as he turned to her. At that same moment heat completely engulfed her.

Piercing blue eyes seemed to stare a hole directly into her soul.

She felt her cheeks warm and was thankful for both her brown skin complexion and the sun's dying rays that hid it from his piercing gaze.

Thick and unruly, his hair fell in discordant silk waves over his head. Although he kept his hair short it was long enough to show that if he allowed it to grow longer, the silken waves would turn to curls.

As if she needed to see that. She thanked God for small favors.

His piercing eyes were the first thing that caught her attention. His skin, a light olive tone due to his Hawaiian heritage, was deepened to golden with the long hours spent in the Hawaiian sun, made for an uncommonly handsome face. The perfection of his features could have been carved from marble they were so precise.

Thick dark lashes framed emerald-blue eyes, and a long nose and sensual lips all completed the picture of a near masculine perfection. A bump on the bridge of his nose, which gave his nose a slightly crooked appearance, prevented his face from being perfect.

But even imperfection made him that much more appealing to her, giving him a more rugged appearance. When one of the women had remarked upon their blue eyes, she'd seen Nick shrug it off with a grin in place, reminding the woman that his and his brother's mother had been half Hawaiian and half white. Although her eyes had been brown, someone, somewhere, had been blue-eyed. DNA had a way of sneaky way of showing up in everyone's family tree.

As Sonia stared up at him, his heritage didn't matter. She only saw the man in front of her. And besides, his DNA made up for a man who was sinfully handsome.

His wide shoulders blocked out the horizon and the setting sun.

Rugged man. That summed up Mr. Keanu Kealoha to a T.

"I'm waiting…Sonia."

Her startled gaze met his. It was the first time in six months of correspondence and three months they'd been filming the show at the ranch and working together that he'd called her by her first name. For nine months he'd called her Ms. Brandon.

He obviously caught her surprise. A slow grin split his face, transforming the normally austere but handsome face into one so breathtaking Sonia feared she would be in serious trouble if he knew his effect on her.

"Sonia?" she asked, putting on a fake careless, teasing smile. "You're sure you can handle calling me by first name?" She could tell her teasing threw him off guard, but he played it well.

He lifted a shoulder. "I figured if you agree, it was about time we called each other by our first names, as we get to know each other better," he said, and brought his hand out for her to shake.

Sonia was looking at his hand as if it was a damn rattlesnake, Key thought, irritated by her reaction. He refrained from his natural inclination to pull back after her obvious distrust, her reaction one he should have expected.

He was not going to allow one small woman to think he couldn't handle her. He kept his hand extended, calmly waiting for her to shake it.

It was way past time that he actually sat down with the woman, got to know her. She was no different than any other woman he'd had to do business... or pleasure with. Although with her, he'd keep it to business.

Despite the way his cock jumped in response whenever she was within "sniffin' distance," as his twin called it. It wasn't as if he was new to dealing with the opposite sex. Whenever he needed an itch scratched, there had never been a shortage of women willing to do the scratching for him.

But that's all he'd ever indulged in. Although his needs ran high, sexually, he made sure any woman he indulged in any...scratching...with knew the score. He did not want a relationship.

Growing up on the ranch had taught him a few things. One was that ranching and the long hours involved to see the ranch a success didn't always work well with trying to have a relationship. But with this woman, he would continue to keep it business as usual.

He glanced down at the sexy producer, who was studiously avoiding his gaze. And something about the woman staring out at this land told him she wasn't the type to get it and quit it, as his brother called Key's infrequent and short-term affairs.

She chose that moment to glance up at him, and Key felt poleaxed.

It was her eyes.

She was beautiful, sophisticated, intelligent and, from the rare times he'd seen her with her guard down, she had a smile that lit up the room. Not that she showed it much around him.

Key felt his jaw tighten. It was his fault. He'd kept a distance between them, he knew, purposefully. But now he needed for her to trust him, needed to keep her close. He'd already agreed to allow them to finish the last few episodes, and with that, the decision to start filming a second season was one he had promised, both to her and his father and brother.

It was a decision he knew would allow him to keep a watchful eye on her so the skeletons in his family's closet didn't find their way on-screen, live and in living color for the whole world to see.

He needed to keep her and her crew around long enough to insure they didn't know his family's secret and use it in some ratings scheme. He had enough on his hands without airing his family's dirty laundry publicly. Especially as he hadn't confronted his father about it, nor told his brother.

He knew time wasn't exactly his friend. He would have to act quickly and earn her trust.

"Does this mean what I think it does, Mr. Kealoha?" she asked, a light entering her beautiful eyes. For a fraction of a moment, Key felt a pang of guilt for his deception. He pushed it to the side. He would protect his family at all cost.

He allowed a slow grin to lift the corners of his mouth. "Yes. I will definitely consider allowing the show to continue—" His last words were swallowed within her embrace as she leaped up and grabbed him, hugging him to her body.

The feel of her small body wrapped around him eradicated every thought from his mind. The reason for the deceit, the very fact that he was deceiving her and had no intention of allowing the show to continue…everything wiped out. Clean.

Hell, he would have a hard time remembering his own name he was so stunned by her reaction.

Without conscious thought or will he drew back and lifted her face, forcing her chin up and forcing her to look at him.

"And I think it's time we drop the formality. My name is Keanu. Friends call me Key," he said and, brushing a finger beneath her chin, he tilted her face farther up so that he could see her eyes.

He saw her throat constrict as she swallowed, biting her lower lip in obvious nervousness, a gesture he'd seen her do on more than one occasion. His eyes followed the trail of her small tongue.

"And can we be that?" she said, her voice husky. "Friends?"

"Yes," he said, hearing the huskiness in his own voice but not giving a damn. "I think we can be that. At the very least," he finished, his eyes locked on hers.

Her startled gaze was centered on him, and as he leaned down and brought their faces together, bringing their mouths into alignment, he slanted his mouth over hers.

Chapter 5

When his lips met hers, shock prevented Sonia from reacting initially. Besides balling her hands into fists placed on his chest, she was helpless to do anything else.

Shock soon turned into temporary pliancy when the sweetness of his lips registered in her consciousness, and for a brief moment she gave into the kiss.

"Hmm." Her soft sigh escaped from behind her lips as he gently laid siege to her mouth.

His lips were hard, unyielding and yet soft on hers. Easy. Inquisitive, yes, but not demanding.

Her fisted hands relaxed and flattened on the granite-hard walls of his chest. She gathered the worn and soft faded work shirt between her fingers and kneaded the material softly. She drew in a moan around his lips and allowed him to bring her closer.

"Hmm." Again, her soft moan whispered between them. Just for one moment more…

When she felt the tip of his tongue feather back and forth, seesawing against the inseam of her mouth, she drew in a hissing breath, which seemed to be the invitation he was both waiting for and needed. Deftly he slipped his tongue between her lips, forging inside to stake his claim.

From there the kiss changed, his hold on her became tighter, more demanding. Even as she tried to shut out that voice of reason pinging away at her brain, she moaned, melting into his embrace, his hot kiss.

When she felt his hands drop from her shoulders, and curve around her backside, the whiny voice in her mind would no longer be denied.

What in hell… Why in hell was she allowing this? She felt like screaming as the internal fight made the deliciousness of what was going on, the hot spur-of-the-moment kiss, dissipate and reality rear its ugly head.

Damn reality, she mentally grumbled.

Sighing, she pushed away from him, creating space between them.

"Keanu, stop," she pleaded, nearly breathless.

She knew the minute reality crashed in on him, as well. No sooner had she shoved away from him, nearly stumbling as she did so, than she caught the string of emotions cross his handsome face. He closed his eyes briefly before running a hand through his dark hair.

"God, I am sorry for that. I don't know what in hell came over me to do something like that," he began, taking a step toward her, one hand extended.

Sonia didn't know whether to be happy, sad or mad at his exclamation. Or what to make of the look of disgust that crossed his face. Was her kiss that awful?

She knew the minute he caught her reaction. Usually she considered herself a good poker player, but as much as she tried to hold her cards close, she feared her true feelings showed. *God, can a hole just open up and swallow me?* she wondered, wanting to run as far away as possible, quickly, in order to get it together. The simple kiss had been as devastating as it was short, too short.

Oh, God, I need help, she thought, feeling the heat threaten to burn her face completely up. Even now she yearned to feel his mouth on hers again.

She took a deep breath and stepped back, away, trying to hide her face, knowing the message *desperate woman* had to be blazing across her forehead.

She did what any woman in her shoes would do: she put a mask over her emotions.

She pursed her lips, frowning, with a look she hoped passed as offense plastered on her face, in an effort to *save* face. After a moment she knew her faux look had been read and interpreted as she'd wanted.

"What was that all about?" she asked tightly.

A sense of relief mixed with regret when he quickly brought his hand down. For a brief moment, she thought she saw disappointment in his eyes.

She kept a tight lock on her face, her body, forcing herself not to go to him, explain that she didn't mean what she'd said.

She stopped herself, barely. He turned away, his big shoulders hunching down. It was long moments before he spoke, but she waited, knowing that the ball was in his court, as she'd volleyed it back to him.

"I'm sorry," he murmured in his deep baritone voice. "That wasn't supposed to happen."

Sonia waited for him to say more. Yes, she knew she could have gone to him, breached the small gap, turned him around and told him it was okay, he hadn't really done anything to her that she didn't want. He hadn't done anything to her that she hadn't been yearning for, for weeks. She could have laughed and shrugged it off as a heat-of-the-moment kind of thing.

Yet she held back, some inner voice telling her it wasn't the way to go. Let him think what he wanted. It was the best thing.

It was bad enough how this guy made her feel, plunging her back to her adolescence as thoughts of him plagued her night and day like some lovesick kid, without him knowing how badly he affected her. Best thing to do was get this over with, play it off, laugh it off, whatever....

He turned to face her. The fake smile slipped and she put it firmly back in place, brightly keeping all feelings firmly on lockdown. When he moved as though to walk closer, she held out a restraining hand. "Look, no need for any more apologies," she said, a breathless laugh tumbling from her lips. "No biggie, we both just got caught up in the moment."

A frown marked his nearly perfect features. "Look, Ms. Brandon, I—"

"Ms. Brandon? Come on, I thought we already agreed...first names." She maintained the bright smile and, with her next words, drove in the nail.

"Hey, after a kiss like that, I'm pretty *sure* we're on a first-name basis." Before the smile could slip she leaned down and grabbed her messenger bag and lifted it over her shoulder. "It's going to be a busy day tomorrow. I'd better go. I'll make sure Patricia gets the new contract for you, your family and your lawyers to look over for the new season."

With that, she quickly spun around, thankful she didn't fall in her haste and finish the night off with a bang to complete the task of making an utter ass of herself. Because it wasn't as if she had done that *at all* tonight.

Holding back the crazy, embarrassed tears and with as much dignity as she could muster, barely a looking over her shoulder, she all but ran away from him. Deciding to forgo heading to her trailer, hoping Patricia had locked up, she lifted the keys from her bag and, before she was even in range of the remote, started jabbing at the little unlock symbol. She couldn't get out of there fast enough.

She hopped inside her rental and, before the car was barely turned on, reversed out of the driveway and was making her way out of the Kealoha Ranch as though the devil himself was after her.

God only knows, after the oddness of the evening and the way the night had turned out, he probably was.

Chapter 6

"Oh, my God…is it true?"

She frowned as her assistant burst into her trailer, a huge grin on the woman's lined face as she approached Sonia's desk. Patricia stopped in front of the desk and clasped her hands together.

Is what true? Sonia mouthed, frowning as she nudged her Bluetooth away from her mouth. Then she made a pointing motion with her finger, indicating she was on the phone.

Patricia's mouth formed an O. She grimaced and held up her hands in apology.

"I'll make coffee!" she whispered excitedly, and turned, briskly walking toward the minute area Sonia had designated as her reception area in the small trailer.

Sonia was in the middle of a conference call with Marty Shop, one of the executive producers for the show. Sonia held back a sigh, wondering how Patricia had found out the news. The only thing she could be referring to was the news that the Kealohas had agreed to do the show.

She hadn't told any of the staff yet, wanting to speak to the execs at the station first before she alerted her staff.

Then there was the matter of actually *getting* the family to sign the contract for the new show.

She felt confident that would happen. The nagging voice in the back of her head, pinging at her, reminded her that she hadn't actually *gotten* anything beyond a vague agreement of a second season from the one family member whom she knew to be the only dissenter.

But what a dissenter he was...without his assent, a second season wasn't going to happen, as she knew neither his father nor brother would agree to it without Keanu's approval.

Sonia brushed aside the inner voice. It had to happen, she knew it would. Despite what had occurred between the two of them. A blush stole across her face. Not that she was using him in any way, as she'd never resorted to that way of doing business. Besides, he'd been the one to initiate the kiss, not her.

"Sonia, we have all the confidence in the world in the show and, most important, in you. From the beginning you've bought something different...

unique, to the show. Your vision has been one of the main components of the show's success. Just keep me abreast of what's been going on and let me know when you need the money!"

Sonia laughed along with Marty Shop. It was no secret that Marty, along with his partner, Sheldon Harris, partners in business as well as life, were two of the most influential, i.e. richest executive producers in the industry.

She and Martin Von Shoppe, which he had shortened and changed to just Marty Shop, had worked together previously, and although he ran a tight ship in the area of finances, when he backed a project, he went all the way. In the industry, having a man like Marty on her side went a long way toward building not only her reputation but also her career.

"Will do, Marty," she replied warmly.

"I'm sure they aren't going for the boilerplate contract they signed the first time, so as soon as you get the details of what they want, send it to legal and we'll start the new contract. But let's not vacillate on this one. They're a hot commodity, honey," he drawled. "We don't want someone else sweeping them off their feet before we get the contracts written and signed!" he finished before disconnecting the line.

She sighed, tapping the end button on her Bluetooth before withdrawing it from her ear. She rubbed at her ear; the pressure from the bud always caused her ear to throb.

She hated to wear the darn things and only did so when she was on important business calls as it enabled her to be hands-free. She had a tendency to nervously walk around while on the phone, something she did when she was either excited or nervous. Both were the case when she was speaking to Marty about the show.

"Was that Marty?" Patricia asked, her gaze direct, and Sonia was unable to hide her surprise.

"You always roam when you're on a call that's important. Kinda figured it was Marty," she replied in answer to Sonia's unspoken question.

"Oh, man, am I that predictable?" Sonia groaned as she accepted the coffee Patricia offered, hedging on whether or not she wanted to confide in her assistant.

Although she didn't want to share the news with anyone before it was a done deal, Patricia was different. She and Sonia not only shared a working relationship, Sonia valued her as a friend, as well.

"Okay, but you absolutely can not tell any of the crew just yet," she stated, grimacing after taking a sip of the coffee. "Remind me to clean that pot out," she groused, and laughed at the impatient look on her assistant's face.

"Okay, the Kealohas have tentatively agreed to a second season of the show!" she said, and laughed outright at Patricia's look of astonishment.

"Are you surprised I got them to agree?" she asked smugly, around the lip of the cup.

"Uh…that would be a yes!" Patricia responded immediately, and just as quickly Sonia saw her pale cheeks bloom with color at her outburst.

"Hey, I'm not sure how to take that!" Sonia set the cup down, the coffee not settling well in her stomach.

"I'm batting zero here, kiddo! I did not mean it that way," Patricia said, and groaned.

"I'm just surprised that they agreed so quickly." Patricia retracted, sitting down in the gray utilitarian chair in front of Sonia's desk. She crossed her legs and took a sip of the coffee. Immediately, she made a face, too. "I guess I need to go back to making your coffee for you. This sucks," she complained, and Sonia threw her a grin.

"Seriously, I understand your concern, Pat. But it's all good," she said, a confident smile on her face as she looked at her assistant.

"So the relationship—on a business level," Patricia hastened to tack on, "is going well?"

Sonia shrugged, bringing the awful coffee to her mouth only to hide her expression. "Yes, it's going well. Of course, we haven't gone over the new contract yet, but the family has agreed to a second season."

"All of them?" Patricia asked, her voice tilting up at the end, in question.

Sonia turned to face her assistant, one brow raised. "Am I missing something here, Patricia?" Although she kept her voice level, Sonia caught the look of embarrassment that crossed Patricia's face.

"Oh, gosh, I didn't mean that in any bad way! Yeah, I'm really screwing up here today! I was… just wondering how everything is going with you and Keanu. Look, I've been working with you for a while, Sonia. It kind of hurts me that you don't feel comfortable enough talking with me about what's going on."

"Okay, and just what do *you* think is going on, Pat?" Sonia asked, infusing a casualness into her tone that she was far from feeling. No doubt she probably came off sounding like a bitch, but at the moment, Sonia didn't care.

Patricia looked at her directly, stood and planted her hands on her hips. "I've been with you for a while, young lady. So, I'm more than aware of how you think. And right now," she said, her voice softening, "you're thinking the world is on your shoulders. But it's not. Well, it doesn't have to be. You know you can trust me, Sonia. What's going on?" she said, and Sonia sighed.

A smile turned up the corners of her lips, even though the last thing she wanted to do was smile.

"I'm sure the Kealohas are all on board. Even Keanu," she began, not sure how to voice something she hadn't really figured out herself.

As perceptive as Patricia was, Sonia knew she'd probably already guessed that she had developed feelings for Keanu, so she plunged ahead.

"I think I've fallen for Keanu. And I don't know that I have objectivity when it comes to how to approach him in business. Everything is crazy for me right now. And I think I might have made it worse," she began in a rush, and once she did, she told Patricia how she felt. She stopped short of telling her of the kiss they'd shared. Barely.

As soon as she unloaded her fears in one rush, she waited for the relief to come.

It didn't.

Instead of feeling as if a weight had been lifted from her shoulders, curiously, depressingly, she felt as though her burden had just gotten heavier. She shrugged off the feeling. She had a tendency to keep her feelings to herself; outside of her parents she rarely confided in anyone what she was feeling.

"I'm sure it will all work out, Sonia. Trust your instincts," Patricia said as she walked to her desk.

Sonia was opening her mouth to speak, to try to take back the disclosure, but she closed her mouth. Biting the corners of her mouth, she reminded herself that it was easier to go forward than trying to go back. Besides, if she had to trust anyone with the admission, she knew no one was more trustworthy than Patricia.

Chapter 7

"Good job, men. Let's call it a day—you all can take off for the night. See you on Monday," Key told his crew, while dismounting from his horse and removing the thick cowhide leather gloves from his fingers before rubbing his hands together.

He arched his back to relieve the pressure that had built up from not only the day but the entire week. Despite the pain in his back from the hard work, it was a pain he'd gladly endure as it helped, minutely, keep his mind on work and off Sonia.

He grunted low in his throat and then placed the gloves into his back pocket, grabbed his hat from the ground and jammed it back on his head.

It had been a long day of mending fences, a thankless but needed job that Key, like most who worked on the ranch, considered one of the most tedious.

When he'd relieved Ailani, his ranch foreman, of the duty, the look of surprise on the young woman's face had been enough to bring a slight smile to Key's mouth.

"Hey boss, no need for that, I can handle the fences. Not much else on the agenda so pressing that I can't handle this task. Bane can oversee the cattle run scheduled this afternoon instead," she'd said, referring to her assistant. She was already in the middle of making one of her infamous lists to organize the day.

Key had held up a hand, stopping her. He knew that if he didn't, Ailani would keep going, assuring him until she turned blue in the face that she could handle it all. He shook his head. The young woman reminded him a lot of himself and his brother when they were her age, not that they were that far apart in age as she'd grown up right alongside him and Nick.

By ranch industry standards Ailani was fairly young to hold the position of foreman, at the age of twenty-eight. But, she was the best damn foreman they could have wished for. Her father had been the foreman for the ranch for many years, working the Kealoha from the time Keanu's father had bought the ranch as a young man, over forty years ago, until last year when Ailani's father had retired.

Ailani had not only grown up on the ranch, she'd worked it from the time she was in her teens. She had attended the University and studied agriculture but soon after had returned to the ranch. She'd worked as her father's assistant, and no one could or had accused her of getting the job because of who her father was.

When her father was prepared to retire, there hadn't been any question as to who would take his place.

And the Kealohas had made sure everyone knew the promotion had been legit.

Although they'd been younger when the affair had occurred between Nick and Ailani, Nick and Key made it a priority that the entire crew was on board, and it hadn't been easy. It never was in the male-dominated industry of ranching, and they didn't want any hint of nepotism to taint their decision so she'd had to prove her worth.

Any thoughts of unfair promotion for the few who were so inclined to think that way flew out the window with the hard work and dedication Ailani put into the job.

"Ailani, I've got this. Besides, you got the job, remember?" he joked, and she laughed, punching him in the arm, the casual gesture highlighting their years-long acquaintance. He laughed. "Besides, I want to do the fencing," he'd said, and she'd laughed again, blush covering her café-au-lait-colored skin.

As he leaned to the side to stretch the tight muscle at the center of his back, he grimaced. He'd thought, at the time he'd switched duties with Ailani, that the hard work would keep him too busy to think of Sonia and what had happened…what *was* happening between the two of them. But it hadn't.

Instead, due to the tedious nature of the job, he'd had his mind cleared to think about her and their situation.

He began to prepare his horse to mount, then paused, turning toward his men.

"Y'all have a great Fourth and be careful out there," he began, his gaze going over the small crew. "For those of you who have the day off, make sure you're extra careful. Don't want to hear about anyone doing anything…stupid this year," he admonished, and Rue, one of the youngest of his men, burned bright red.

The young man ducked his head and nodded toward Keanu in deference. "Yes, sir," he said, taking the mild rebuke in stride. Several muffled laughs met Rue's words and he flipped off one of his buddies who'd laughed.

Key ignored the laughter as well as the rebuttal, taking it all in stride. Working with men…that was all a part of the game.

Every year he gave a briefing to his men whenever the Fourth came around. He typically gave the younger ones the afternoon off, as it seemed to be one of their favorite holidays. Although for the younger men and tourists around the island the Fourth was highly anticipated; for Key, his brother, father and the senior ranchers, it was just another day. However, at night they usually put on a miniature fireworks display.

The Fourth of July was a busy time for tourists on the island, and in particular the small town close to the Kealoha Ranch. The small island got most of its income from tourists and the ranch business as well as the fruit orchard his family helped to maintain.

Although he and Nick had lived their entire lives on the ranch, they were close with their outside community, having gone to elementary through high school with most of them, as well as attending the university with those who had stuck around the mainland after graduating from high school.

"Hey, boss, I'm supposed to head out with the family this weekend, is that still going to be okay?"

Key turned to face one of his young ranchers, Bane. As Ailani's assistant, Bane was one of the men who usually stayed around when others were given time off. It worked for him, particularly as he, like Ailani, lived on the ranch.

However, the young man had recently gotten married to his high school sweetheart and started a family, his youngest just a newborn, his oldest only two years old. Key had allowed the small family to live in one of the cottages on the ranch. Bane's parents hadn't seen his newborn son as they lived on one of the neighboring islands, and were coming up for the holiday.

"No problem, Bane. As long as you get your mother to make me some of her famous haupia coconut pudding," Key asked, and Bane laughed along with him. Bane's mother once worked on the ranch in the kitchen, cooking for the men. During the holidays she would always make Haupia coconut pudding, a cultural tradition, and would set aside a heaping portion for Key.

"You bet, Key, no problem. She'll love to!"

Key clamped him on the back, "Good thing, man. Have a good one," he said, and for a moment felt envy for his friend.

Married with children was the way most of his friends had gone, early on. While some had gotten married right out of high school, those who'd gone to university had waited until after acquiring their degree.

He and Nick, at the ripe old age of thirty, were two of the oldest in their age group to still be single.

Key doubted that would ever come for him, the whole married-with-children thing. Happily ever after and everything that came with it wasn't high on his list of things he believed in or a state he aspired to find himself in.

"Oh, shoot, man, almost forgot." Bane turned as he was preparing to leave and, leaving his horse tied to the post, jogged back over to where Key was standing.

Key frowned as he watched his friend dig a note out of his back pocket and hand it to him.

"What's this?"

Bane shrugged, turning to go. "Don't know. One

of the stable boys handed it to me, asked if I could give it to you today. Came from one of those Hollywood folks," he replied, giving the generic name they all gave the crew from the show.

"Why in hell didn't he just give it to me?" Key grumbled, but flipped open the paper to read the contents.

His jaw tightened, a contemplative look coming over his set features as he read the note.

Let the games begin.

Chapter 8

Key marched his way through the formal dining room, his booted feet hitting the wood flooring, the sound echoing and rebounding off the walls loudly in the quiet house.

Didn't appear that anyone was home, which was a good thing. After the day he'd had, he wasn't in the mood for idle chit damn chat.

Would like to meet with you to discuss our agreement. On a personal level. Anytime, anywhere…

Sonia's message on the note he'd been given days ago was firmly stamped in his brain. Since then, he'd made it a point to ignore her until he figured out her game. He wasn't in the mood to make a dumb-ass mistake with a woman.

He made his way toward the kitchen and tossed his hat on the large granite counter before throwing open the refrigerator and grabbing a bottle of beer.

He'd worked the men on the range hard, as they'd spent the greater part of the past two days mending fence. It was a job he usually allowed the foreman to oversee, using the hands to help fix the miles of fence, but this time he'd taken on the task himself.

And if he had his way, he'd spend the remaining days the film crew were to be at the ranch on that task, as far out of reach as possible. After his last explosive meeting with Sonia, he didn't trust himself to be alone with the woman. He didn't trust himself not to make good on his last promise to her. After reading the note, he didn't know which was worse, his decision to use her in order to find out what she knew, if anything, about his family, or her apparent need to use him.

Anytime, anywhere... The last line in the note echoed his mind. He tightened his jaw and yanked open the fridge.

He was in the process of grabbing another beer when Nick sauntered into the room. Damn, he was hoping to have the house to himself for longer than ten minutes. He eyed his brother warily over the neck of the bottle, but otherwise ignored his presence.

"Looks like the crew is doing a good job of fulfilling their end of the bargain, don't you think, bro?"

"Man, don't even go there," Key replied tightly. "And don't think I don't know you're responsible for that little setup this morning," he finished.

Nick threw up his hands in feigned defeat. "I don't know what bug crawled up your ass, but I'm sure Mahi has something that'll fix you right up, bro," he said, and laughed at the single-digit salute his comment garnered. But when Key continued to ignore him, his face set, the smile slipped from his twin's face.

"Hey, seriously, I don't know what you're talking about, Key!" Nick exclaimed, his thick brows pulling down into a frown once he realized Key wasn't exactly laughing back.

"Aw, come on. You're not even going to give me a clue?" he cajoled, shoving his body away from the column he'd been leaning against and making his way toward his brother.

When Nick reached out to grab the beer on the counter, Key ignored him, opening the refrigerator door again to replace the one Nick had filched.

Key didn't give his brother a glance, simply popped open the bottle and threw back his head, allowing the dark amber to slip down his throat. What use was it, anyway, he thought—it wasn't as if Nick would admit he'd been the one to throw him to the wolves.

"Family first, Nick. Always. Setting me up like that? That was bullshit."

"Okay, seriously, what the hell are you talking

about?" Nick asked, all signs of humor completely gone from his blue-eyed gaze as he stared, frown in place, at his brother.

"Dinner will be ready soon, boys, make sure you're washed up!" When their housekeeper, Mahi, bustled inside the room, he broke the tension and Key leaned back against the counter, his eyes closed, and polished off the beer.

"What is going on in my kitchen, boys? You know I do not tolerate any foolishness. You two had better not be fighting again!" the old man admonished. His words brought a ghost of a smile to Key's face. Although both he and his brother were long past the age of being "boys," Mahi was as much like family as their own father, as neither twin remembered a time the elderly man hadn't been around.

He'd begun as a stable hand but, after realizing he wasn't able to keep up with the job, their parents had invited him to come and help take care of the boys. He still referred to them as "boys" whenever he was irritated with them.

"So, you want to tell me what the hell is wrong with you?" Nick asked, coming to stand less than two feet away, not wanting Mahi to overhear them.

"You're seriously telling me you don't know?"

"Hell no. What gives?"

Key sighed, his gaze going over his brother's, looking for signs of humor.

He'd been wrestling with the contents of the note he'd been given earlier. After he'd read the contents, he'd at first been amused, before realization dawned on him. He'd tracked down which stable hand had given Bane the note, and from there it hadn't taken long for him to find out who'd given the boy the note. Assuming it had been Sonia, he'd been surprised to find the note had come from his brother.

But why would his brother play messenger? Had Sonia spoken to him about their encounter?

Without further ado, he opened the note and showed it to Nick. Nick's glance fell over the crumpled piece of paper and, after scanning the contents, a grin split his face.

"Oh-oh-oh, brother, looks like you and the pretty producer—"

"Stop right there. First off, why the hell would you play messenger? What did she tell you?"

"Messenger? Tell me what?" The look of confusion was so real Key knew that, as talented a prankster as his brother was, he was telling the truth.

"You really don't know about this?"

"'Fraid not, bro, I had nothing to do with this. Didn't it come from Sonia?"

Key signed, refolding and placing the note back in his pocket. "Yeah, apparently. But according to Bane, he got it from the stable hand, who got it from one of the guys working the south field, who got it from—"

"From the milkman?" Nick laughed but sobered quickly at the scowl on his twin's face. "That's a hellafied mixed-up version of telephone, Key. But, I wasn't involved in the mix-up," he said, referring to the children's game. Quickly his scowl cleared. "I gave one of the kids a note to give to Ailani about the fencing. I thought she was going to be mending fence today, anyway, not you. Maybe that's the mix-up."

"Hmm. Maybe. Anyway, why not just call her instead of a note?" Key asked, relieved that his brother hadn't been involved, and trying to steer him away from asking any further questions about the note and Sonia, now that Key had inadvertently divulged the information, something he would not have done had he not thought his brother was involved.

He was still trying to figure out the situation himself and didn't need his brother's advice or ill-timed humor.

"Cell phone? We're talking about Lani, here," Nick replied with a laugh, walking over to the large oval table in the eating area of the large kitchen.

It was a well-known fact that Ailani was a throwback to an earlier generation. She was one of the few people he knew who didn't carry her cell on her person twenty-four/seven. The fact was, if she could get away with it, she wouldn't own one at all.

Key grunted in agreement, conceding the point. "Yeah, I guess the old-fashioned way of communication is the best for her."

"Okay, now that that issue is resolved…what's up with you and Sonia?" his brother asked, grinning hugely, ignoring Key's immediate reaction.

"That's not up for conversation," Key replied before bringing the bottle to his mouth and drinking.

After a few moments he finished and slammed the bottle on the counter, and opened the door again for a second.

"Guess I don't have to ask what kind of day you had, son?"

Hearing his father's voice, Key paused, slowly turning around to face the elder Kealoha. "Hey, I didn't hear you come in. How you feeling today?" he asked, concern replacing the short-tempered tone in his voice. He watched as his father walked in, the ivory-handled cane thumping against the hardwood flooring with every step. It was all Key could do not to race to his father's side, take his cane and help him into one of the large, comfortable, high-back kitchen chairs that circled the table.

He glanced over at his brother, knowing Nick was thinking the same thing he was, and also that to do so would anger their father.

Alekanekelo Kealoha was a proud man.

Since the stroke, he'd been forced to accept help he'd never had to in the past. Now, as he was rarely seen outside his personal living quarters, they didn't want to upset him by running to his side to offer help he didn't ask for.

His father's pride was another reason he had yet to approach him with what he knew about his and Nick's heritage, who their biological father was and why his parents had kept it from them.

Warily Key watched his father walk farther into the kitchen, relying heavily on his cane.

He grabbed two more beers and walked over to the table where his father was standing, near Nick. After offering his brother one, he held out the other to his father.

When his father accepted the drink, all three men sat down at the table.

The elder Kealoha took a drink and placed it down carefully. A frown marred his aged but handsome face as he glanced first at Key and then Nick.

"Before I go into finding out what in hell is going on with my boys...stop looking at me like I'm gonna break. I'm made from tougher stuff than this watered-downed crap they pass off as beer these days," he said, grimacing, his glance going over the bottle he held in his hand.

"No damn wonder. Light beer? May as well get me a bottle of milk," he griped, yet brought the bottle to his mouth and finished it. "Can't wait to get back to my brewery."

A look passed between Key and Nick. They knew their father was feeling better if he was ranting about beer. The man was a self-proclaimed aficionado of all beer and had been brewing it from the time they were small boys.

They hid their grins.

"So what gives...what's going on? And don't tell me 'nothing,' I know something is going on. And it sure in hell is something more than that crew running 'round here causing the disharmony."

After making the pronouncement he pierced each man with a stare.

The humor dropped away, and Key held his tongue. Although Alek Kealoha hadn't been working as much as he used to before the stroke, Key knew their father was as aware of what was going on at the ranch as when he was fully working it.

"Is it something going on with the production crew? Seemed like that was doing fine. The exposure for your mother was the reason we all agreed. But I know that she wouldn't want that at the expense of the ranch," he said, and Key felt guilt stab at him. It wasn't the show that was the problem.

It was the things he wanted to do with the producer that was the problem.

Damn.

"Far as I'm concerned, the crew is the least of the problem. I think you need to ask Key what the problem is." Nick was the first to speak, ignoring the glare Key sent his way.

"What, man?" Nick said. "All I know is that for the last few months you've been acting like something crawled up your butt you didn't like, and—"

"*Nothing* could crawl up my butt that I'd like, bro, let's get that straight. I'm not into all that kinky shit you seem to—"

"I have a feeling it has something to do with more than the film crew. I think our shy kid here has a crush on—"

"And I sure in hell haven't been called a 'shy kid'

since I *was* a damn kid. If you got something to say, *bro,* spill it. If not, you know what you can—"

"Enough." The one word brought the brothers' heated words to a halt.

While the verbal exchange was going on, Alek Kealoha sat back, crossed his big arms over his chest and watched his sons going at it like two rabid pit bulls.

He sighed. "What in hell is going on around here? *Really* going on," Alek asked, and glanced up as Mahi chose that moment to begin bringing over the evening meal.

"I've been asking them the same damn thing, Alek. Can't seem to get to the bottom of it. Tension so thick you could cut it with the back end of a rusty hoe," the old man groused, and, before anyone could say anything in rebuttal, he placed the food on the table and turned away.

"Maybe you can do something with them. Been like this off and on for the better part of a week. I'll turn these knuckleheaded boys of yours over to you, gladly." He grumbled and left the kitchen, with all eyes on him.

Alek gave them each a look that brought back memories to Key of when they were young boys and were about to get in deep-shit trouble.

Which was more often than not, he thought and glanced over at his twin. They exchanged a look, one that told him his brother's thoughts were the same as his.

Yes, things had been tense lately, Key acknowledged that, but he and Nick usually worked it out, and nothing major had happened they hadn't been able to handle.

He held his brother's gaze for a moment before turning to look at their father.

"Looking good, Dad. Glad to see you up," Nick said gruffly, but Key heard real emotion in his brother's voice, one that he shared.

Key observed their father and tried to hide his surprise and joy at the sight of him at the table, obviously ready to join them for dinner.

The times his father came and ate with them for dinner had been few and far between since their mother's death nearly a year ago and his father's subsequent stroke.

He and Nick exchanged another telling glance... Mahi had roused their father out of bed on the pretext of "taking care" of the "boys."

Both men hid their pleased grins.

"Now look here, no matter what it is, we're family. And family—"

"Takes care of family," Key and Nick murmured together.

"It's good to have you eating at the table with us for dinner, Dad," Key said, and smiled at his father, gritting his teeth together to force away the sudden emotion.

"Yeah, well, it's about damn time, I guess. Can't keep moping around forever. Your mom would kick my rear end if she knew." He stopped, his voice thickening with emotion.

"Yeah, she would," Nick replied, his voice rough.

Alek looked from one to the other, cleared his throat and clapped his hands together. "Okay, well now how 'bout we dig in. Looks like Mahi outdid himself," he said, and both men laughed. Although he was a sentimental man, their father was, when at his best, succinct in both action and words.

He gave them a questioning look, but they simply shook their heads and, after a silent prayer of thanks, dug in to the feast Mahi had prepared.

Key put the quandary of what he would do about the note…the invitation, to the back of his mind to contemplate later.

Chapter 9

Sonia stared at her reflection, examining her body.

She carefully moved the lapels of her robe to the side and, with hands loaded with cream, swiped her hands over her breasts and down the length of her body, slowly.

When she came to the juncture of her thighs, she paused, one hand brushing over the low curls that covered her mound.

Biting the corner of her mouth, she feathered her finger over her clitoris, imagining it was another's hand doing the caressing.

She stopped before she could go any further, her face burning with color.

"God, what am I doing?" she asked aloud. She turned on the faucet and quickly washed her hands, drying them on the hand towel she'd grabbed after the shower.

It wasn't as though she was embarrassed to touch herself—she was an adult woman. It was simply that as she began touching herself, images of another's big hands in the place of hers came to mind, and she knew to continue along that thread was a recipe for disaster.

Especially as she was set to meet up with her would-be fantasy lover in less than an hour.

With a deep sigh, she closed the ties to her robe firmly. She reached up and, using the ends of her robe, wiped away the dewy moisture left over from the steam of the shower on the mirror before plopping down on the small, tufted chair and examining her face.

Any other time, for any other date, she wouldn't be putting herself through this drill. Although it had been a while since she'd gone out on a real date. Immediately the thought rang in her mind—is this what this was, a real date?

Sighing, she reached for her moisturizer, squeezed a generous dollop on her hand and smeared it on her face, her mind going over exactly what had brought her to this time.

After the kiss she and Keanu had shared, she hadn't known what to expect the next day. Would he be cold to her, as was his normal MO, ignore her and act as if it didn't happen, or would he seek her out and pick up where he had left off, and take the intimacy to the next level. Or somewhere in between.

What he'd done instead had completely shocked her. Normally they rarely saw each other, besides occasional glimpses, during filming. She hadn't known if it was by accident or design that it happened that way. But when she hadn't seen him at all the next day she'd felt a sting of disappointment, one she tried to brush aside and pretend didn't exist, but it refused to go away.

The next day she'd been given a note from one of the stable hands, from Key.

Name the place and time. If lunch works best, let me know. If not, I know of an out-of-the-way place we can meet for dinner. Either way, doesn't matter to me. ~ Key.

Succinct and to the point. What the hell was she supposed to make of that, anyway? Was that his way of asking her out to eat? Was it a date? she'd wondered, frowning as she reread the brief note. Then it dawned on her that perhaps it was simply to go over the contract, and she felt all kinds of stupid for thinking otherwise. The kiss hadn't meant a thing to him.

Damn him. She shouldn't feel this way about him. Shouldn't give a damn if he wanted to pick up where he left off, shouldn't care that it had all been some game with him. Her only thought should be getting his signature on the contract. And if that was what he wanted, that worked for her, too.

To that end, for the rest of the day, she'd firmly put Key and her confusing feelings for him out of her mind. Told herself to keep it business and nothing more. To do anything else was a surefire way of getting hurt.

After careful consideration she'd sent him a text agreeing to the date, and he'd given her the name of the restaurant to meet him.

Sighing, she reached for her under-eye cream and lightly dabbed it on the undersides and corners of her lids. She considered her reflection in the mirror. Although she never considered herself a raving beauty, after having worked in the entertainment industry for a number of years she was convinced that she could hold her own. What did he see when he looked at her? Did he find her attractive?

"Why do I even care?" she murmured aloud as she dusted her face lightly with powder before applying her makeup. "I'm beyond ridiculous."

Still, she took extra care with her makeup. She lifted the dark pencil to outline her lids but hesitated as her hand hovered over the gold eye shadow. She glanced over her shoulder to look at the gold kimono hanging on the outside hook of the closet. Dare she wear something so overtly sexual?

She stood and padded over to the silky dress and pulled it from the hanger, spinning around to examine herself with it in front of her body.

Her mother had bought the dress last spring while she and her father had been overseas, filming a documentary in Japan. It was authentic and beautiful. She'd tried it on once and found that not only was it those things, it also fit her body like a second skin. Laughing, she'd placed it at the back of her closet, knowing she'd never dare wear something so form hugging.

Yet she'd brought it with her to Hawaii.

Even as she'd packed the dress, she'd had Keanu in mind, as from the beginning, even though she hadn't met him, he'd already begun to filter into her thoughts often.

She was tempted to put it away and wear something a little less sexy, less…revealing.

Either way, doesn't much matter to me. Something about that phrasing had set her teeth on edge.

As though she didn't matter. As though she made no impression or had any lasting effect on him.

She smiled.

Let the games begin.

Chapter 10

Sonia arrived at the restaurant they'd decided on, a place she had never been to, but one that he'd chosen, called the Mai-Kai, and as she closed and locked her car door, she carefully made her way along the stone path leading to the wooden porch and opening to the restaurant.

From the outside the establishment, the place appeared to have seen better days. Looking like a rundown old building in need of repair, she took in the shabby appearance with a wave of disappointment. Obviously he hadn't given much thought to where they would eat.

With tension playing havoc on her nerves she'd stepped inside, only to be pleasantly surprised at what she encountered the minute she entered.

Authentic Polynesian decor tastefully accented the large dining area. Complete with authentic and detailed beautiful wood carvings and various maritime antiques, the atmosphere was both classic yet casual, a tasteful blending of both.

A smile lifted the corner of her mouth as she glanced around, searching for Key. When the maître d' approached her and asked her name, he held out a hand, indicating that she was to follow him as he led her to a perfectly stationed table, hidden away from the main floor.

Key stood as she approached and pulled out her chair. As she walked over to where he waited, her eyes drank in the sight of him, just as he was returning the favor.

He could have stepped out of any one of the shows she produced and fit right in. Tall, his body would look good in anything, but the casual slacks he wore clung to his long muscular legs, the silk shirt open at the neck exposing a fine dusting of hair on his chest.

When he smiled at her, she blushed, embarrassed to be caught ogling him so openly.

But when she caught the admiring look in his eyes, part of her embarrassment melted, and she gave him a genuine smile in return.

"I'm glad you made it," he murmured, and her gaze flew to his, wondering at the wording, but she simply smiled in return.

"Glad you made it, as well," she replied. When her stomach growled she groaned, laughing lightly.

She hadn't eaten since breakfast, so busy with the day and fixating on what she would wear to the date that she'd been a mass of nerves.

"And now that the pleasantries are over, are you hungry?" he asked, completely deadpan.

When she looked his way, she saw the small lift of one corner of his mouth and, for some reason, the small humorous quip had helped to break the ice.

"I hope you don't mind but I placed our orders for dinner."

When she asked what he'd ordered he told her he wanted to surprise her, give her a sampling of what Hawaiian food had to offer.

She took a sip of the ice-filled goblet and hummed in appreciation. "What drink is this?" she asked.

"It's pineapple iced tea. I took the liberty of ordering that for you, as well. If you prefer I can order you something else," he asked, and she waved a hand, shaking her head no.

"This is delicious," she said, smiling up at him.

He returned the smile. "Glad it meets with your approval. I also ordered appetizers," he said, and, as though on cue, the waitress came over with a platter in her hand, placing it down in the center of the table.

"I had no idea this would be such a feast!" she said, rubbing her hands together, a grin splitting her face.

"And this is only the appetizer," he said, and she groaned, but the grin remained.

When he'd asked where she'd like to go, she'd

said she wanted something local, but local for Hawaii was unlike any other place in the world, as it was a mixture of cultures with Portuguese, Chinese and Japanese cultures highly influencing their food.

Before her was a veritable smorgasbord of exotic foods on the large, pretty platter.

She had an idea of what some of the dishes were but turned to Keanu to find out about the rest of the food.

He smiled slightly as he pointed out what the dishes consisted of.

"What is it, exactly?" she asked, staring down at the good-smelling yet odd-looking assortment of delicacies.

"You're going to love it. This," he said, pointing to one of the white, flaky, steaming buns on the platter, "is manapua, which comes from our Chinese culture—char siu. It's barbecue pork in a bun," he said, lifting one of the steaming buns and breaking it open.

Sonia closed her eyes, inhaling. "Smells divine," she said.

"Tastes even better. Wanna give it a whirl?" His voice was husky low.

Sonia opened her eyes to find his gaze on hers. She glanced down at the roll in his hand, the offer to eat from him one she couldn't resist.

Leaning forward, she took a bite, allowing the sweet juice to stream down the corner of her mouth.

His finger dipped, caught the juice on the tip of his forefinger.

She watched as he brought it to his mouth and licked the juice away.

"Delicious. Just like I knew it would be," he replied.

Oh, God, she felt her heart drop and her gut seemed to hollow out at the simple yet intimate gesture.

She blew out a long breath, forcing a break in their connection.

Just like that, he had her. The man did things to her like no one ever had.

Suddenly shy for no apparent reason, she swallowed, forced a bright smile on her face and, with a shaky finger, pointed to another appetizer. "And this one?" she asked, clearing her throat. "What is this?"

She glanced up at him from beneath lowered lashes to see the familiar, sexy, small smile play around his mouth.

"This one is nori maki sushi rolls, from our Japanese heritage. It's vinegar rice with tuna, shrimp flakes, egg, carrots, gobo all rolled in nori and sliced. Want to try this one, too?" he asked, the light in his eyes challenging as he deftly picked up the chopsticks and lifted one of the rolls onto it.

She straightened her back, lifted a brow. And smiled.

She knew he expected her to say no.

Which is exactly why she leaned forward and opened her mouth for him to feed her.

When she moved to take him up on his challenge, Key bit back the groan. God, the woman was turning him on even as she ate, tempting him to not only lick the sauce that dripped down her sweet, full lips but to take those lips and give her the kiss he'd wanted to give her since he'd seen her walk into the restaurant earlier.

When she'd entered, looking like sin wrapped in the skintight gold-colored silk kimono, she was a gift he wanted to open. When he'd glanced down at her small feet in the stiletto heels, the ends tied in a bow around her slim ankles, she definitely was a present Key wanted to unwrap.

He wondered how he'd kept his cool and not carted her off to the nearest hideaway to see what lay beneath the sinfully wrapped present. From head to toe, the woman was gorgeous.

He was used to her hair being straight. When she was on set, she wore a ponytail, positioned at the back of her head.

But for tonight she'd left it loose. The normally straight strands were a riot of natural wild curls that cascaded down her bared shoulders in the sexy dress that hugged and outlined each one of her scandalous curves.

Damn.

She'd used a light touch when it came to makeup,

as she normally did; however, she'd paid close attention to her beautiful almond-shaped eyes, deftly outlined in a soft shade similar to the color of her dress.

The cut of the dress gave ample attention to her generous breasts, outlining and lifting them, emphasizing their perfection, making his mind race with thoughts of peeling the material to the side to get a small glimpse of what lay beneath, what she kept hidden from his view.

His cock hardened at the thought.

He glanced over at her, keeping the smile away. He hadn't thought she'd go for it again. Thought he'd scared her into chickening out. Despite himself, his admiration for her seemed to keep on growing.

He quickly reminded himself what his mission was. He was the seducer, not the other way around.

He brought the roll to her mouth and watched as her small, white, even teeth took the entire roll in her mouth, gently, thoughtfully chewing before swallowing.

"You're right. It is delicious," she said. "As delicious as anything I've had in a long, *long,* time," she finished, a small dimple appearing in her cheek.

Key ignored the way her quirky smile, the one that was as much a part of her as her humor, came out after she made the quip. He ignored the way it made his heart seem to thump harder against his chest.

Before he could say anything more, the waitress brought them the main meal. He sat back in his chair, feeling as if he'd just been run over by a steamroller, more than glad for the interruption.

It was getting to be where he was second-guessing who was the seducer and who was the one being se-duced.

Chapter 11

When the main course arrived, Sonia's face lit up. "So much food...it's like thanksgiving!"

"This one I'm sure you're familiar with," he began, jumping right in with explanations. She grinned—if she didn't know better she'd swear he was enjoying his food tour as much as she.

"It's seasoned mahi mahi, a pelagic fish. Next to it is fried nenue, another tasty fish, but this one is eel," he said, using a fork to lightly pierce the flesh. "This is laulau, which can be pork or chicken—in this case the Mai-Kai used chicken. And this piece is a butterfish wrapped in taro leaves, held together with ti leaves and steamed." He paused, brought a small mouthful to his lips and took a bite, his eyes closing. "And the best fish you'll probably ever have," he said, and Sonia's eyes darted to his mouth and throat as his strong column worked the small bit of food down.

She forced her eyes away and focused her attention on the food. She caught but ignored the knowing look that passed over his face. "Continue," she said, waving a hand over the food.

He inclined his head briefly. "I aim to please," he murmured, and their glances caught and held. It was she who broke away this time. He cleared his throat, continuing. "Sweet-and-sour spare ribs, beef stew and poi, a Portuguese bean soup, round out the rest of the meal."

She sat back, her eyes wide, taking it all in.

"Oh, my…" she murmured, her mouth watering as she glanced at the food. "Why did they bring us so much?" she asked.

Keanu grinned. "It's just a sampling of each, not full servings. Besides, I wanted to make sure you got the full…flavor of the island. Didn't want you to go away…unsatisfied," he said, and her eyes flew to his.

She got the impression he wasn't exactly talking about food.

"And for dessert, we will bring you our famous kulolo," the pretty waitress said, dimpling as she returned to the table. "It's made primarily from mashed taro corms and coconut milk." She stopped and frowned, considering the dessert, then snapped her fingers. "It's kind of like a pudding, or fudge. Tastes like caramel, you'll love it!" she enthused, and

Sonia smiled, knowing the young woman had given the description for her sake, as Keanu no doubt knew of and had eaten the dessert many times before.

"I make it myself. My mother handed the recipe down to me, from generations," she finished with a look of pride crossing her young face. "Please enjoy!"

At that moment Sonia's stomach growled loudly and she glanced up and caught his grin.

"Hungry?" he asked, a small smile playing around the corner of his sensual mouth. The incredible spread before her was completely forgotten briefly.

"Yeah, you could say that."

Their glances held, and had it not been for their waitress bringing a fresh pitcher of the delicious, tinkling, pineapple iced tea, Sonia feared she would have made a complete and utter fool of herself by hauling him over the table and feasting on him instead of the meal in front of her.

She felt heat warm her cheeks at the thought. In addition to his other talents, she hoped like hell the man wasn't a mind reader, or she was in serious trouble.

"Do you like what you see?" he asked, and she nearly groaned but kept it together. Without looking down, she nodded her head.

"Do you?" she asked boldly, and was rewarded when she saw his reaction to her words. A flicker that came and went in his light blue eyes.

"You could say that," he agreed huskily.

Again the moment stretched out before them. It

K-ROM-13C

We'd like to send you two free books to introduce you to Harlequin® Kimani™ Romance books. These novels feature strong, sexy women, and African-American heroes that are charming, loving and true. Our authors fill each page with exceptional dialogue, exciting plot twists, and enough sizzling romance to keep you riveted until the very end!

HARLEQUIN KIMANI ROMANCE...
LOVE'S ULTIMATE DESTINATION

OUR FIRST

JUDY LYNN HUBBARD

Beneath Southern Skies

TERRA LITTLE

To Tame a WILDE

Kimberly Kaye Terry

Truly Yours

THE BOUDREAUX FAMILY

DEBORAH FLETCHER MELLO

Escape

JANICE SIMS

Your two books have combined cover price of $13.00 in the U.S. $14.50 in Canada, but are yours **FREE!**

We'll even send you two wonderful surprise gifts. You can't lose!

THE EDITOR'S "THANK YOU" FREE GIFTS INCLUDE:

Two Harlequin® Kimani™ Romance Novels
Two exciting surprise gifts

YES! I have placed my Editor's "Thank You" Free Gifts seal in the space provided at right. Please send me 2 FREE Books, and my 2 FREE Mystery Gifts. I understand that I am under no obligation to purchase anything further, as explained on the back of this card.

PLACE
FREE GIFTS
SEAL
HERE

168/368 XDL F5DC

Please Print

FIRST NAME

LAST NAME

ADDRESS

APT.#

CITY

STATE/PROV.

ZIP/POSTAL CODE

Thank You!

BUSINESS REPLY MAIL
FIRST-CLASS MAIL   PERMIT NO. 717   BUFFALO, NY

POSTAGE WILL BE PAID BY ADDRESSEE

HARLEQUIN READER SERVICE
PO BOX 1867
BUFFALO NY 14240-9952

If offer card is missing write to: Harlequin Reader Service, P.O. Box 1867, Buffalo, NY 14240-1867 or visit www.ReaderService.com

NO POSTAGE
NECESSARY
IF MAILED
IN THE
UNITED STATES

was as though the two of them were alone in the crowded, popular restaurant.

"I'm glad we did this," he said, and she nodded her head.

She wiggled in her seat, rubbing her hands together, her attention diverted to the delicious array of food in front of her.

She glanced up in time to see Key trying to not show the grin on his face, but she waved it away. "Laugh all you want!" she said, one side of her lips kicked up in an unrepentant grin. She held three fingers, ticking them off as she spoke. "One, this looks good. Two, I'm starving like Marvin. Three, I haven't eaten since breakfast and a certain person left me hanging for lunch, and, four, did I mention this looks absolutely divine?" she asked, and laughed outright when she heard his low chuckle.

She had just taken a bite of the flaky white mahi mahi when she heard a rusty-sounding laugh from Key.

Surprised, she quickly chewed the fish and looked at him. "What?" she asked, after swallowing.

"Nothing," he said, the smile lingering. "I'd better eat in case you finish it off before I can even get my napkin open," he said, deadpan, the humorous glint in his eyes making her laugh.

As they continued to eat, the conversation flowed smoothly, with rarely a moment of silence. By the time the meal was complete, Keanu had never known a moment where he'd felt so relaxed in the company of a woman.

"And when he *and* the dog both began to howl to 'Atomic Dog,' in harmony...I lost it. Game over," she said, her laughter bubbling over and contagious. She'd been regaling him with stories, or Hollywood horror tales of the wannabe rich and famous, as she dubbed it, sharing the story of the time she'd helped her best friend, Dee Dee, in a casting session to pick contestants for a new game show. Not only was she hilarious in the retelling, but her humor was contagious and Keanu found himself actually laughing out loud several times throughout the evening.

As she laughed, exposing her beautiful white teeth, he bit back a groan.

God, she was gorgeous. She looked good enough to eat, and although the conversation was kept light, easy, he'd had a hell of a hard time not staring at her mouth the entire time. As she ate with gusto, enjoying her meal, his mind played tricks on him, images and thoughts of what else she could do with those pretty, full lips of hers playing hell on his mind.

As she leaned back in her chair, a satisfied look on her expressive face, he bit back a groan. He wanted to be the one to give her that look.

Every time that thought surfaced, he ruthlessly pushed it down. He was with her only to gain information and nothing more.

But he hadn't been prepared for how utterly charming she was.

Although they'd communicated often before, it had always been business, and though he'd caught glimpses of a more carefree Sonia, nothing had prepared him for this. Funny, beautiful and sexy. Damn, she had it all. And with each moment he spent in her company he could no longer fool himself that he had agreed to the date to keep the enemy close.

He noted that she hadn't brought up the contract once during the conversation, and he placed the ramifications of that fact in the back of his mind for later consideration.

For the moment, he wanted to enjoy…her.

"Oh, God, I could go on and on," she said, lightly giggling. She glanced over his head, saw the clock above the wooden tiki totem and covered her mouth with her hand, one eye closing as she grimaced. "I've been talking nonstop! Why didn't you stop me? Once I'm on a roll, I never stop," she said with a grimace. "I must have bored you to death!" She groaned, and he shook his head.

"No, in fact, it was the exact opposite. I don't know the last time I've had such a good time. Who knew the job of hotshot Hollywood producer could be so, uh…" He paused, not sure how to phrase it.

"Crazy?" she filled in. "Sometimes that's the simplest way to put it!" She laughed before sobering, pinning him with a stare. "What did you have the waitress put in this drink? I'm spilling my entire life story and you haven't told me anything about you, Keanu."

"Nothing much to tell. You pretty much know my life story, don't you? With the film crews around there isn't much to hide. Besides the whole mistaken-for-my-brother episode, that happens more times than I want to share," he said, shaking his head.

"Come on, there's got to be something more. Something you can share with me. It'll be just between the two of us," she replied lightly.

He raised a brow. And just like that, his earlier suspicions came to mind. Did she know that his mother had had an affair with one of the richest ranchers in the United States? And if so, what did she plan to do with the information?

He kept his reply light. "Maybe if you stick around long enough, I'll share all my family's dirty laundry. But for now, would you like to dance?" he asked, as the band that had been on break returned to the stage.

Standing, he walked to her side and held his hand out for her to take.

Sonia glanced down at his hand and placed her palm inside his without hesitation. The minute the band had set up and the music began in the softly lit restaurant, she'd wanted to dance with him. But the conversation had been so good she'd quickly lost track of time. Then she noted the change in him once she asked him to talk more about himself.

Sonia knew she had said something wrong the minute the light dimmed in his blue eyes and his features, once relaxed, stiffened. But when he asked her to dance, she glanced at his face and saw the genuine warmth reflected inside.

Gladly she had placed her hand in his, and allowed him to lead them to the small dance floor.

When he brought her body close to his, she kept her hand in his and the other around his waist. With their nearly foot difference in height, she knew it would be awkward at best if she tried to place her arms at his shoulders.

He didn't seem to mind; in fact, he drew her nearer and swayed lightly with her in time to the surprisingly bluesy number the band was now playing.

"Ranching was the only life I knew. The only life we'd been brought up knowing," he began, his head low as his chin lightly rested against the top of her head. She drew in a breath when he began speaking, glad he couldn't see her face, as she knew it reflected her surprise when he spoke willingly about himself.

He spun her around lightly, deftly avoiding contact with another couple who'd joined them on the dance floor.

As she listened to him talk about growing up on the ranch, her body completely relaxed into his.

As they danced close, she felt him gently rub his chin back and forth against her hair while they moved as one, as though they'd been born to dance this way together, on the dance floor.

This close to him, his natural musky, masculine scent reached out and grabbed her, pulling her into its heady embrace, and she shamelessly went along.

Nuzzling her body close, she inhaled deeply. Not only did he look good, he smelled so incredibly good.

Sonia loved a man who smelled good.

And his scent was so appealing to her that her nipples beaded beneath the silk kimono. Held this close against him, she wondered if he could feel them against the wall of his rock-hard chest. When he brought their joined hands, which lay in between them, tighter against his chest and squeezed, she knew he had.

She didn't care, because just as he was affecting her, she was doing the same thing to him. Sonia smiled when she felt the hard edge of his shaft behind his slacks nudge her lower belly, stifling a groan at how good that felt, as well.

Oh, God, if she'd didn't get away from him soon, there was no telling what would happen, and all of her good intentions to leave it as just business would fly right out the window....

He chose that moment to tilt her head back, and with his thumb, he forced her to look into his eyes. She caught the flash of hot desire within, a desire that matched her own.

It felt good to finally be in his arms.

"Come home with me."

It felt right to have her in his arms. As Key stared down at the beautiful woman, he could no longer deny the attraction...the off-the-charts chemistry they had going on. And he no longer would.

For now, tonight, he would take what fate had offered him on a beautiful, luscious platter. As for her agenda for him, long-term, he didn't give a damn.

Not tonight.

Chapter 12

Sonia gazed up at Key as they made their way toward his home, her heels clicking loudly, seemingly too loud, against the stone pathway that led to the house.

Nervously she looked around, wondering who, if anyone, was up at that time of night.

"No one is around the ranch," he murmured, his hand beneath her elbow as they walked toward the side door, the one he'd told her led to his separate suite of rooms.

"The men who live here, their quarters aren't on this side of the ranch, Dad is asleep and has been since this evening, and Nick is… Hell, who knows where Nick is." He glanced down at her as he flipped open the keypad and swiftly pressed a series of numbers and opened the door, allowing her to enter in front of him.

Once inside she followed him in the dark hallway until they reached a door and he opened it, again allowing her to go in front of him.

The tension was thick with the knowledge of what she…what they, were going to do. What they'd both agreed, without verbal assent—to end their night together.

Yet for all of that, nerves attacked Sonia. She felt his presence directly behind her in the dark room and drew in a deep breath, holding it.

When she felt his lips fan the outer corner of her ear, that sensitive spot no other man seemed to have found, her stomach hollowed out.

Hot, forbidden anticipation ripped through her, strong and fierce, until she felt every nerve on edge.

She waited for him to turn on the light, say something…do something, and nearly cried out loud when she felt his big hands settle on her shoulders and pull her body back against his.

"There's nothing to be afraid of, Sonia. I promise I won't do anything to you that you don't want done." He made the promise in a low, deadly sexy voice, the minty breath again blowing against her earlobe.

"You trust me, don't you?" he asked, and after a brief hesitancy she nodded her head.

His hands moved down her arms until he'd reached the underside of her breasts and he cupped them through the silk dress. Her heart stopped completely, and she had to force herself to breathe.

She had never felt like this before, and he'd barely touched her.

She suddenly stiffened against the feelings he was generating, fear beginning to sweep over her.

When he swept a hand down inside the V of her dress, the air lodged in her throat, clogging it, and she released it in one long whoosh of air as his fingers deftly worked their way inside the next-to-nothing bra she wore.

Her groan was long, harsh, and she heard his light masculine laughter. She licked lips gone dry and shoved at his hands, embarrassed that he found humor in her response.

"I…I don't think this was a good idea, Key, I—" His finger stopped her speech and he turned her around to face him. He lifted her chin, forcing her to look at him.

"You affect me like no other woman has. I'm not sure what this is between us, Sonia, but trust me, you're not alone in how you feel," he said, and the sincerity of his words struck her directly in her heart.

"But, as badly as I want you, just say the words and we can stop. I will never force you to do something that you don't want to do," he promised, and brought her hand up to meet his lips, delivering a soft kiss in the palm of her hand that had her melting on the spot.

She swallowed and nodded her head.

When he began to glide the sleeves of the dress down her arm, a shiver ran over her entire body, the beginning of an uncontrollable need making her tremble.

Key was impatient with the feel of their clothes. He pushed the straps of the silk dress down her arms, past her body to pool at her waist.

He leaned back simply to look at her, his gaze centered on her firm, high breasts, the erect, tight little buds of her nipples pushing with insistence against the thin fabric.

With a groan, he unhooked the front clasp and splayed his fingers across the soft brown globes, one at a time, and felt his hands shake.

"You are so beautiful. Please, don't hide from me, Sonia," he said when she glanced away from the heat in his eyes.

He leaned down and laid siege to her lips. Devouring them, he kissed her with a zeal that bordered on desperate.

"God, your mouth is sweet. If your mouth is this good, I can't wait to see how good the rest of you tastes," he said after long, drugging kisses that left his cock harder than ever, and her lips full and red.

Although it was dark, he knew his words had somehow embarrassed her as she ducked her head away.

"Hey," he said, forcing her to look at him. "We'll take it slow as you want, I promise," he said, his voice low. "But I want to explore every part of you, every inch, every curve," he said, and again stroked a hand over her breasts, making her nipples ache and crave for his return when his fingers drifted away.

He kept his gaze on hers and captured one brown, turgid nipple in his mouth and suckled it, while he used his hand to play and toy with its twin.

With reluctance he pulled away from the sweetness of her breasts and ripped his shirt in half in his haste to get it off before he tossed it to the floor. Swiftly he unbuttoned his slacks, unzipping them enough so that his cock, hard and ready, could find some relief from the too-tight confines of his pants.

Not giving her time to think, he lifted her in his arms and strode though his sitting room, kicking open the door to his bedroom. Once inside he carried his bundle toward the center of the room and gently deposited her on the bed.

He joined her there, immediately going back to work on her breasts.

He heard her heartfelt mews of pleasure and felt her arms wrap around his neck, tugging him closer. He obliged her and, after switching sides, greedily latching on to the other perfect breast, giving it as much attention as the first.

"Oh, God, Key…it feels so good," he heard her say, the huskiness in her voice turning him on even more, his cock so hard he felt as though he'd release before he even entered her if she kept on moving against him the way she was.

He needed to see her. Reaching over, he turned on the bedside lap and instantly the small light gave an amber glow to the room, and his eyes sought hers.

She was the sexiest thing he'd ever seen.

The glow from the light accented her pretty brown body and his breath caught in his throat at the picture she presented, with her bra hanging halfway off her body and her dress pooled around her waist. Her hair hung in loose waves around her beautiful face.

He kept his face on hers as he slowly finished undressing her, the act itself erotic, somehow forbidden.

He watched her as she licked her lips, her head slightly down, her eyes lifted, watching from hooded eyes as he undressed her. He smiled lightly. Nudging her, he encouraged her to lift her body so that he could ease the dress the rest of the way down her body and, drawing it from her, allowed it to drop on the floor beside the bed.

She lay before him, wearing nothing but the sheer bra and a scrap of lace, the small triangle barely covering her pretty pussy from him.

He fingered the silk aside and inserted his finger inside, and saw her breath catch at the decadent act.

"Do you like that, Sonia?" he asked, and she nodded her head wordlessly.

He kept his gaze on hers and lowered his head, his mouth and lips replacing his fingers. At his first touch her body arched high from the bed and she cried out.

"Keanu...wait, please, wait...I can't take it," she

said on a harsh moan, her body mindlessly grinding against his face, and he felt a purely masculine satisfaction.

He held on to her hips and continued his assault. As he licked and stabbed against her slick folds, he inserted a finger into her opening and her walls immediately clamped down and tugged.

He drew his mouth away to look at her. "God, you're tight," he said, his cock hardening to granite as his fingers continued to press inside her clenching walls.

He leaned down between her legs again, and this time he separated her folds and exposed her clit to his gaze. He slowly drew the bud deep inside his mouth and sucked.

Sonia nearly came apart.

At the first contact of his mouth on the most secret part of her body, she held her breath.

Although she'd experimented sexually, she'd never allowed a man such an intimacy with her.

In fact, she'd never actually experienced full lovemaking, a fact she knew if Key were aware of, he would stop.

But God, she didn't want him to. She'd never felt anything so incredible before. And she was helpless to stop what he'd…what they'd started.

She closed her eyes and allowed the orgasm she felt to burst free, her body spasming even as he continued his oral sensual attack. Her body was no longer hers to control.

Spent, she could do nothing but lie down, her head lolling to the side, a smile of satisfaction on her face. When she felt the bed move, she opened an eye to see him opening the side table drawer, and, although she couldn't see him, the telltale sound of foil ripping brought her eyes fully open and her body into a sitting position.

"We're not done by a long shot."

She swallowed. She knew she had to tell him. Tell him before he found out and it was too late.

She feared he would stop what she so desperately wanted him to finish.

With her gaze locked on his, she watched him as he stood and swiftly finished undressing; his body unclothed was a pure work of art.

His long legs were thick with muscle, his thighs so hard they looked as if they could choke a horse.

And what lay between his tree-hugging legs would make any stallion envious. His cock lay long, thick and curved against his stomach, the triangle of dark wavy hair nestled around it, covering part of his heavy sac drawn tight against his body. Her eyes traveled up the rest of him, past his tight six-pack abdomen and up to his chest, where his nipples peaked erect through the light pelt of hair.

Her eyes moved to his face, and the light of desire in his vivid blue stare that watched and waited for her perusal, allowing her the time to absorb the moment even.

He was the picture of masculine beauty.

Keeping her gaze, he slowly, methodically, placed the condom over his shaft, his long thick fingers deftly and efficiently working the latex over his massive length.

Sonia felt hot liquid ease from her body at the simple act.

When his body covered hers, she gladly accepted the weight, her mouth eagerly seeking the haven of his. The kiss went on so long that by the time it was over, her body was on fire with need.

But she had to tell him before it was too late.

When he took her mouth with his, again, all else but the feel of his mouth and body covering hers went out of her mind, and she gave in to his touch.

Chapter 13

He couldn't get enough of her. As he kissed her, he knew it was time.

He gently eased one finger inside of her and again, her walls clamped down on him. Then he frowned when he met a barrier.

Key broke the kiss, his breath coming in harsh gasps as he pushed her away, far enough so he could see her face. The low light from the small lamp bathed the room and Sonia in a golden glow, her heated gaze fixated on him.

"Sonia…have you ever…?" He allowed the sentence to dangle, and when he saw her swallow and slowly close her eyes, he knew that, as unbelievable as it was, she had never made love before.

It all hit him at once. She was giving him something so precious…the very meaning of it all was crashing down every wall he'd tried to erect between them.

Hollow walls, he now knew. He brought a hand up to run a finger down the side of her face, then he looked away from her and rose reluctantly from the bed.

"God, I want you," he said, simply turning back to face her. She held his gaze. He wanted to rip off the remainder of her clothes and make love to her, give her what she—what her sinful body—was asking for. "But I can't do this."

The words were torn from him and he pushed away from her.

"Please." The soft entreaty came from kiss-swollen lips as she stared at him, her liquid brown eyes asking him to give them both what they wanted.

"Are you sure you want to go through with this, Sonia?" he asked, afraid to hear the answer but knowing that if he didn't ask now, soon it would be too late.

She swallowed and kept her gaze on his. Lifting herself onto her knees, she crawled to the edge of the bed and stopped when her body was close to his.

She leaned out and took his hand, guiding him back to her. With a groan of acquiescence he allowed her to bring his much larger body down, until he blanketed her body with his own. He settled into the V of her thighs, the warmth from the center of her femininity resting against the rougher cotton of his boxer shorts.

"Yes, Key. I've never been so sure," she whispered. "Make love to me."

He wanted her. Wanted her so badly he felt as though if he didn't have her soon, he'd lose it. But still he wanted to make sure. He couldn't promise her anything. It was sex and sex only.

He ignored the mocking laugh that accompanied the thought.

"You know that this is just—" His voice trailed off. Hell, he didn't even know what to call it.

She smiled in the low light. "I know. And that's okay, Key. Just make love to me." Her voice broke. When she grabbed his hand, brought it between their bodies and moved it down until it rested against her silk-covered mound, he groaned harshly.

That was all he needed to hear. He removed his shorts and intense desire took over.

He lowered his head and covered her mouth with his, grabbing and tugging her bottom rim fully inside his. God, he loved the taste of her mouth.

As he kissed and nuzzled her mouth, he gently moved her hand away, grabbed the other hand and planted both high above her head, while with the other he covered her mound. Her tight little moans of delight filled his mouth as he continued his oral assault.

With a groan, his mouth hungrily devouring her lips, he lightly fingered her mound, brushing the pads of his finger back and forth over the low-trimmed, light springy hair, playing back and forth against the seam of her vagina, teasingly, until she cried and moaned against his mouth. He broke away to see her face.

"Do you like what I'm doing to you, Sonia?" he asked, her labored breaths matching his. He needed to ready her for him. Without conceit he knew he was nowhere near a small man, a fact that she would enjoy a hell of a lot more if she had more experience sexually.

Even when he'd been a virgin, he'd never made love to a virgin before.

She nodded and he saw the way her jaw worked. She swallowed.

His eyes trailed down to the crests of her breasts, and he gazed in fascination at her dark nipples, tight and erect.

"Yes, I can see that you do," he murmured, and bent his head down, capturing one of her nipples deep within his mouth.

He laid her back down on the bed and, starting at her mound, kissed and caressed his way up her body, pausing occasionally to deliver a kiss…or bite…along the way.

When she hissed after one of his stinging kisses, he growled low as he immediately saw the cream of her arousal seep down her leg.

By the time he reached her face he took it between his hands and sexed her lips as he planned to do with the rest of her body.

"I want your first time to be special. But you have

to relax. Okay?" he asked. When she nodded, he smiled and used the pads of his fingers to scrape across her clit and test her readiness.

When his fingers came back soaked with her own dew, he knew the time had come.

Slowly, inch by inch, he fed her increments of his shaft until he came against the thin barrier. He took both of her hands within his and covered her mouth with his as he raised her hands high above her head,

With one final thrust he embedded deep inside, his mouth swallowing her cry at the final invasion.

He waited until he felt her muscles relax and her sheath slowly calm the frantic pulsing on his shaft.

"Are you okay, baby?" he asked, and she smiled.

Their tongues met slowly at first until mutual need and desire soon overwhelmed her. He pinned her hips lightly and began to thrust.

Once he was assured she could handle him, the strength of his thrusts grew stronger until her helpless cries of pleasure filled the room.

He knew she would need more in order to release.

He freed one of her hands and eased it between them, found and captured her bud and worked it in time with the power of his thrusts.

With each drag and release Sonia felt her body give in to the erotic pleasure Key was delivering with every stroke.

She hadn't known what to expect and thought the

pain of the first time would eclipse the pleasure, but she'd been wrong.

After the first pain had subsided, her body, so wet and ready for him, began to adjust and accept his thrusts as she clung to his body.

On and on the pleasure went, spiraling though her body, washing over her, as her cries rang loud while she accepted his loving.

Tears fell trickled down her face, the pleasure was so intense as she accepted his heat. Her body was liquid fire, and she needed to come so badly she felt near to explosion, yet it remained out of reach.

Frantic, she ground against him, his hard, thick shaft hitting the back of her walls until he felt the top hit her spot.

"Oh," she keened in a tight, high voice, her body going up in flames. At the same moment he hit her spot, his talented fingers pinched her clit and she screamed so long her throat grew painful, her voice hoarse as the orgasm swept over her, deadly and direct.

Before long she gave in fully to the release she felt hovering, her mind and body utterly and completely relaxed.

When she felt his arms circle her body and draw her close, she closed her eyes and, with a smile on her face, slept.

Walk away before it's too late....

As he watched her sleep, the thought crept into Key's mind. And just as soon as it did, he rejected it.

He'd not planned any of this, hadn't sought to seduce her and hadn't meant to make love to her.

His hand came out to smooth away an errant curl that clung to her sweat-covered brow.

And most definitely he hadn't planned to be the first man to make love to her.

But now that it had happened, he was damned if he was going to walk away from it, from her. At least not yet. Not until he explored this incredible... chemistry...between them.

Chapter 14

"Is it my imagination or does my butt look very... large in these jeans?" Sonia spoke to the trailer at large as she examined her figure in the new jeans she'd bought but had yet to break in.

She'd barely had time to get dressed that morning after the long night spent with Key, a night she knew she'd never forget.

Even now a blush stole across her cheeks in remembrance.

Would he want a repeat performance? she wondered aloud, still examining her figure. Or had she scared the heck out of him after he realized he was her first? She sighed heavily.

She'd left early, not wanting anyone to find her in the house, still unsure of where the two of them stood, despite the intimate night and the things he'd shared with her, things she cherished more than he could know.

After the first session of lovemaking, they'd slept for a few hours, but when she felt his shaft, hard and thick against her backside, she'd sleepily turned over and wrapped her arms around him, and he'd gently made love to her again.

Afterward they'd spoken softly, sharing small stories of their lives growing up.

She'd confided the reason she'd gone into television. As the daughter of two award-winning parents who filmed documentaries about cultures around the world, she'd grown up with a love for film, although she hadn't gone into the field her parents had.

She'd also told him that, although she'd traveled with her parents, she'd always felt as though she were the odd man out.

"Why was that?" he'd asked, his fingers feathering back and forth over her exposed arm, and she sighed, leaning back into his embrace.

"Hmm. I don't know," she said, and gave a feigned nonchalant shrug of one shoulder. "They always seemed as though they didn't need anyone else but each other. I came late in their lives," she began, and laughed. "'Unexpectedly' was Mom's way of putting it. They were already in their forties by the time I came along, and they had decided *not* to have children." She laughed without humor. "Imagine their surprise when I arrived."

"I'm sure it was an unexpected but wanted surprise for them. I couldn't imagine anyone *not* loving you," he'd said, and her heart seemed to skip a beat at his wording.

She continued. "Well, I don't know that I was always quite what they expected. They took me with them, but I never felt at home. You know what I mean?" she'd asked.

He hadn't answered immediately and she thought he'd fallen asleep. When he spoke she startled, as she'd began to doze off.

"I do, in a way. Know what you mean about not being accepted. It's no secret that my brother and I don't exactly look like what you envision someone of Hawaiian heritage to look like," he began, and Sonia held her breath. She'd never seen a picture of their mother, but had assumed they looked like her, as they looked nothing like their father.

"We got teased as kids. But we could handle it. We were always the tallest, the strongest, so if some ass thought we'd cower from being bullied, they *always* learned the hard way the error of their ways," he said, and Sonia shuddered. Both Key and Nick were not only tall but held a natural muscularity, one she had no doubt left them bully-free as children.

"Nick and I have always known our family history is…murky. Even though Mom was half Hawaiian and half Anglo, the blue eyes we have didn't come from her side of the family, as far as we know. And neither did they come from our father."

"Is your father's parentage mixed?" she asked hesitantly.

"No." The answer was abrupt and she regretted asking the question. "No more so than anyone of Hawaiian descent."

"I'm sorry, I didn't mean to pry," she said softly.

She heard his indrawn breath before he brought her closer to his body. "It's okay. You didn't pry. It's an honest question. The answer isn't easy. And…it's something I've been dealing with lately."

His big body tensed, and Sonia *felt* him hesitate, as though he wanted to say something more.

When he remained silent, she didn't press.

The fact that he'd opened up to her showed her that maybe there was more to them than wild chemistry and sex so hot her panties grew wet just thinking about it. Just thinking about him.

She'd woken up to hear him in the shower and had decided to make her not-so-grand escape, leaving before he came out. She'd quickly gathered her things and hightailed it from his room, nearly running to her car in her haste not to be seen.

Despite self-avowals to the contrary, wherein she assured herself she was a grown woman and could make love with whomever she wanted…and spend the night, the thought of someone seeing her emerging from his room was one she wasn't prepared to deal with.

But she knew she'd have to deal with it. They both

would. They hadn't exactly spoken about where they went from there.

Oh, well. She knew she'd have time enough to think of all of that today as she doubted she'd see him.

She twisted her body so that she could see herself more fully in the oval mirror attached to the back of her thin office door, even though her mind was far from what the mirror showed her.

"Your butt…and every part of you, looks perfect from my angle."

Sonia nearly leaped a foot in the air as she spun around to find the source of the voice, nearly tripping on her own feet in the process. Her eyes widened to find Key standing in the doorway, his heated stare focused solely on her ass.

"Oh, God, did you hear me complaining?" she asked, groaning as she adjusted her T-shirt, subtly covering the waist of her jeans, as she'd lifted it away to examine her hind end.

"I did. And like I said, from my view, you have nothing to worry about," he replied, and walked inside the room.

Sonia's eyes widened as they took in him, her body tingling in immediate remembrance of last night and what he'd done to…and with her. Just like that, her panties dampened and she felt heat rush to her face.

Her gaze first went to his face, cataloging features that seemed to be indelibly imprinted on her brain.

His expression was set, unreadable. She wondered if her leaving so early had upset him, or whether he had been grateful for the reprieve.

His jeans were old, naturally faded and molded his long legs to perfection, and the boots he wore were scuffed. The shirt was a plaid, frayed work shirt, the ends cuffed up past his elbows to reveal the fine sprinkling of dark hair on his arms.

The same dark hair that Sonia knew, from first-hand account, covered his stomach, abdomen and upper thighs.

Suddenly the room grew warmer, and she felt dizzy. The heat overwhelmed her and made her stumble the slightest bit. Feeling ridiculous that the very sight of him put her off balance, she tried to catch herself, her hands reaching out blindly to grab on to her desk.

Immediately he was there to catch her, and his big warm hands cupping her at the elbows caused a direct volt of electric heat to travel from the point of contact throughout her body.

"Hey, be careful," he admonished, his deep voice low, sexy, washing over her like warm rain.

She glanced up, her heart thudding. "Thank you," she mumbled before she coughed, clearing her throat. "I've been all thumbs today. Guess I'm off a bit," she finished, and could have bitten her tongue out.

Why couldn't she be the calm, cool and collected one, as he was? she wondered. She swallowed and licked lips gone completely dry. Putting as much distance between them as she could, she walked to the far corner of the room.

With shaky hands she grabbed a cup and glanced over her shoulder.

"Can I get you some coffee?" she asked, raising the mug.

When he shook his head, saying nothing else, his enigmatic stare piercing, she nervously turned away. Busying herself with the coffee, she turned only to find him within a foot of her. She allowed him to take the hot cup of coffee from her. In the state she was in, she would only burn herself through clumsiness.

Her tongue licked the lower rim of her mouth and his gaze seemed to focus on the telling gesture. He kept his eyes on her mouth for long moments before they sought her gaze.

"Why did you leave this morning without telling me?" he asked, his voice low, his light blue eyes direct.

"I—I didn't think it would matter. Keanu, I thought you wouldn't care—"

"Well, I did. And I do," he interrupted, and she swallowed down the lump lodged in the center of her throat, thrown off guard by his ready admission.

He bent low, his warm, minty breath fanning over the side of her ear. "And didn't I tell you my family...and friends call me Key?" he asked, and lightly kissed the side of her throat. Her low, drawn-out hiss of pleasure accompanied his question.

Before giving her time to answer, she felt the sting

of his teeth as they latched on to the small lobe of her ear. Surprised, she arched her back, her body sinking closer to his, her eyes closed as the little pain caused a flood of moisture to pool in her panties.

She swallowed deep. "Uh, yeah…you might have mentioned that once before," she finally replied, holding her breath, waiting to see what he would say…do to her next.

He played it cool, really cool. But after last night, she knew he was anything but. When he brought her close, his hands going to her bottom to pull her closer, she felt the hard edge of his erection.

She closed her eyes, a slight smile on her face.

Within two feet of the woman and he was groping her like a teenager getting his first taste of ass.

Despite his decision to cool it down with her, to let her know that although they'd made love last night he was in no position to offer her anything but what they'd already shared, he found himself hunting her out today, needing to see her.

Needing to touch her.

To say he'd been surprised that he'd been her first had been putting it mildly. Even now the memory of how tight she was, how sweetly she'd clenched and hugged his shaft, brought a painful ache to his groin.

When he'd walked inside her office and seen her checking herself out, he'd been torn between humor and erotic thoughts of what he'd like to do to that sweet butt of hers. She had what his brother once called nice ATW—ass-to-waist ratio. Her small nipped-in waist had been perfect for his hands last night as he'd stroked inside of her.

He held back a groan as he nibbled on the lobe of her ear.

He placed his hands around her waist, and drew her nearer to the part of him that ached the most to feel her. When her soft bottom nestled his erection, he groaned again, tightly.

Damn if he wanted to figure all of that out right now. Right now, he just wanted to feel her. Taste her…

He lifted her by the waist and set her on the desk, laughing low at her "oomph" of surprise.

"Keanu—Key," she began, huskily correcting herself, "wha-what are you doing?" she asked, her voice a sexy, breathless sound, one he knew he was the cause of.

His intention had not been to seduce her when he decided to come to her trailer, but instead to back off. After last night he didn't want things to go any further until he was sure her reasons for making love hadn't been for the show.

The thought of her betraying him and his family was something that plagued him as he was still unsure of her loyalties.

But now, thoughts of betrayal imagined or otherwise, were far from his mind.

He inhaled her unique scent deeply and murmured, "At least I know you want me for more than money."

She laughed, lightly punching him in the chest. "Yeah, speaking of that, I got ahold of the legal department and they're drawing up a new contract for next year," she said, breaking away from his hold and walking over to her desk.

His eyes narrowed as he followed her, his jaw tightening with anger.

"This is just the first draft, and please feel free to take it to your family, have them look it over and—" He grabbed her arm and squeezed lightly, halting her words in their tracks.

"That wasn't what last night was all about, was it?" he asked, his eyes carefully studying hers for a reaction, hoping to see, or not—he was still torn about that—a culpability of guilt in their chocolate-brown depths.

She slowly pulled her arm away, a scowl pulling her brows together. "What are you talking about?" she asked slowly.

"Don't act shy. I'm sure you're not new to this… there was no need, anyway. I would have made love to you, with or without the contract," he said, not certain himself why he said the words, some impulse to get her to admit to something.

When he saw her face tighten, her jaw clench in reaction, he regretted the crass question immediately.

Damn.

Chapter 15

His words began to register in her consciousness and when they finally did, she broke off the kiss, shoving against his chest so hard she made him stumble, surprising him.

She stared at him, her breath coming out in strangled gasp.

She couldn't believe him.

Absolutely couldn't believe he would say something like that to her, much less think she'd be capable of that.

The thought dawned on her, saddening her, that for all the respect she had for him, obviously he didn't return that same respect for her. She fought back the emotion that came with the realization.

"Is that what you think? This is all a part of some

game, that I went to bed with you for you to sign some stupid contract?" she spit out, disgusted with him, but more disgusted with herself for getting so caught up in him that she hadn't seen him for what he was—an insecure jerk with a chip on his shoulder.

"The question is, *Key*," she said, emphasizing his name, and his eyes narrowed, "not what do I want from you…but what exactly do you want from me?"

His jaw tightened as he glared at her. One part of him wanted to show her exactly what he wanted from her; the other wanted to walk away and leave her and the situation alone, order her to get the hell off his land…out of his life, before things got more complicated than they already were.

Damn her for twisting his gut up in knots.

"Get out. Just get the hell out and forget the damn contract. I wouldn't work with your ass if you were the last damn Hawaiian rancher, what the hell ever, on the earth!" She screamed the words, not caring if she was making any sense or not. She wanted him out, before the tears she was barely holding at bay fell. The last thing she wanted was for him to know just how wrapped up she was in him, how his careless words hurt.

"Just get ou—" The rest of her angry demand was caught in his kiss.

She struggled in his hold, determined not to give in to him despite her traitorous body and its immediate betrayal of her.

He held on to her, laying siege to her mouth until she sighed, her body going limp as she moaned into his mouth. Finally he released her. Placing his forehead against hers, he whispered.

"Forgive me. I shouldn't have said that. I know it's not true," he said softly.

Still, the sting of his words hurt deeply.

She turned away, trying to hide the tears but knowing it was no use. He had to know by now how hopeless she was around him. She refused to look at him. "Please…just go."

"I can't."

The words caught her off guard. She turned slowly, eyeing him warily. What trick was he up to now?

"I can't, because if I do, I know I'll be making a dumber mistake than the one I just made. Please, Sonia. Forgive me. I…I want this, whatever it is, to work. I know it's not going to be easy. We'll find a way to separate the business part of our relationship from the personal. Please," he said when she tugged her bottom lip, still unsure.

When she finally agreed, he lifted her in his arms and turned with her, ready to seal the promise with a kiss. Pinning her to the wall, her legs wrapped around his, he softly ground into her, groaning harshly as she responded in kind, rotating her hips against his shaft as she returned his kiss, stroke for stroke. He broke the kiss and stared down at her, his nostrils flaring.

"What we do, on a personal level, is simply between me—" he bent to capture the rim of her lip and tugged it deeply into his mouth before releasing it "—and you." As he lowered his head to kiss her, the sound of a door banging open had them springing apart, and Patricia walked inside.

Her glance fell back and forth between the two, a sly smile crossing her face as she caught the look of wary guilt cross Sonia's face.

"I, uh…didn't know you were otherwise occupied, Sonia. I'll come back at a more…convenient time, hmm?"

Wishing for a timely hole to open up so she could fall in to it, Sonia smiled weakly at her assistant, wildly thinking of something, anything, to say about what she'd just seen.

She came up with nothing.

Keanu glanced at Patricia, his handsome face devoid of any telling expression. "You might want to knock next time, Ms. Haynes," he said before turning to Sonia, pulling her into his arms and kissing her fully on her surprised mouth.

"I'll see you after quitting time. Come to the house for dinner," he said, and turned on his booted heel and strode from the room, leaving an open-mouthed Patricia staring after him and a ridiculous, happy grin on Sonia's face.

Chapter 16

"Beautiful out here, isn't it?"

Startled, Sonia turned when she heard a voice behind her.

She had not expected anyone to be out so late, and neither did she really want anyone to connect the dots and realize that if she was out here at this time of the night…correction, morning, then odds were that she hadn't gone back to her hotel last night.

Again.

Not that Keanu was trying to keep it some deep dark secret, she thought with a grin.

When she saw that it was Ailani, she relaxed and forced a smile of what she hoped was welcome to her face.

"Yeah, it is. Beautiful, that is," she replied softly.

Sonia turned back around to face the orchard, raising her face up to the moon and allowing the slight breeze to blow across face. The smell of hibiscus and fruit in various stages of bloom from the orchard hit her senses as it blew with the wind.

"I love it out here, too. It's where I come to think," the other woman disclosed, coming to stand next to Sonia.

Sonia's head turned enough so that she could make eye contact with her.

In all the time she'd been at the ranch, the few occasions she'd actually spoken to the foreman...or forewoman, as the case was, had been few and far between. When the crew had first come to the ranch they'd interviewed many of those who worked the Kealoha. The young woman who was newly promoted to the rank of ranch foreman was an angle Sonia and the director had wanted to really explore, as they both agreed it was yet another twist to an already unique situation.

Yet after the initial interview it was clear that Ailani Mowry wanted nothing to do with either the show or Sonia.

When the director had approached the Kealohas about her, they'd been told in no uncertain terms that *anyone* who worked the ranch did not have to agree to be on the show.

Although Sonia knew there was a story behind the reserved woman's refusal to be on the show, even in passing, they'd had no choice but to respect her decision, as well as her privacy.

The only thing she had learned about the foreman was that her father had once held the same position and that she had both worked and lived at the Kealoha from the time she could walk.

"You know, when you all first came to the ranch, I was really pissed off."

"Excuse me?" Sonia said, her eyes widening at the woman's choice of words. She hadn't been sure what to expect from her early morning visitor…but that certainly hadn't been it. "Uh…care to explain that?" she asked, at a loss what to say.

Something of what Sonia was feeling must have shown on her face, because she laughed outright.

"Oh, God, that came out pretty rough, huh?" she said, and began to chuckle. "I'm so sorry. Being around guys as much as I am has a habit of wearing off on a girl. Blunt is the only way they do it around here!" she replied. "Please, forgive me!

"Okay, let me start all over again. Hi, my name is Ailani Mowry and I have a tendency to blurt things when I'm uncomfortable."

With a remnant of the smile still on her lips, she struck out a hand for Sonia to shake. An answering smile on her face, Sonia replied, "Hello, Ailani, my name is Sonia Brandon and I sometimes talk to myself when no one is around," she replied, deadpan, and both women laughed.

The tension dissolved and the ice was broken.

Both women leaned against the fence, sharing a companionable silence for long moments. Deciding to go out on a limb, Sonia faced the other woman.

"You know, when I first saw you interact with Nick and Key, I was…jealous," she said, forcing the words out.

"Oh, yeah? Why?" the beautiful woman asked, arching a brow. "Or are you just getting back at me for my earlier faux pas?" she asked skeptically, and Sonia smiled, shaking her head.

"No, I'm serious," she replied, and turned back to look at the orchard.

She reached out to pick one of the abundant hibiscus flowers from the overhanging branch. She brought it to her face and inhaled, thinking.

"I thought you had a…thing going on with one of them."

Ailani laughed out loud, her beautiful white teeth gleaming in the night. "Oh, Lord, *everyone* thinks that at one time or other about me and the twins, I swear!" She realized how that sounded and held up a hand. "Not me and *both* at the same time!" Again, she groaned when that sounded even worse.

Sonia laughed out loud, too, unable to hold back the humor.

"Seriously, Nick and Key are like brothers to me. There may have been a time a while back when Nick and I might have had a thing going, but…" She shook her head, shrugging a ghost of a grin on her full mouth. "Nah, but that was a long time ago. These days the only thing I have time for is the Kealoha. Never leaves me lonely, always there when I need her. She's the best friend and lover I'll ever need," she quipped, but behind the pleasant facade, Sonia caught a glimpse of something more, something the woman kept hidden.

She smiled across at Sonia, and Sonia returned the smile, choosing not to dig into the hidden glimpse she spotted beneath the surface. Maybe one day the two of them would become close enough friends that the other woman would feel comfortable disclosing more.

Even as she thought that, Sonia realized that her time at the ranch would end soon, and she and Ailani would probably never be afforded the chance to form a lasting friendship.

The thought was depressing. Soon, her time with Key would be over. She sighed and pushed the gloomy thoughts away.

"What about you? Apparently more than the Kealoha…ranch that is, brought you out at this time of morning. I'm guessing you stayed last night," the other woman said bluntly.

Sonia laughed. Well, so much for not digging into each other's business.

As soon as the words escaped, Ailani's lighter brown face flushed a dull red.

"God, I'm so sorry. Remember my introduction?" Ailani said on a groan. "I swear 'the one who blurts things' should be my new moniker," she said, and closed her eyes, both hands covering them in her embarrassment.

Sonia laughed out loud, the slight tension completely evaporating again.

She could really learn to like this woman, she thought.

"Girl, it's okay! Really," she began, and stopped before she laughed again. "Hey, it's not like it's that big of a secret, what with me wearing the jeans I had on yesterday and Key's shirt," she said. Surprisingly Sonia felt none of the self-consciousness that she would normally feel given the situation.

"In answer to your question, yes, I did spend the night here," she said, and although she didn't say the obvious, that she and Key had spent the night together, she knew the other woman was fully aware of that.

While she didn't exactly flaunt their relationship, Key had never made it a secret that the two of them were involved.

"And, like you, I came out here just to think. Key brought me here a couple of days ago to show the orchard to me," she said, bringing the flower to her nose to inhale.

The other woman leaned over the wrought-iron railing to snag a flower, as well.

She toyed with one of the petals, her features thoughtful. "When we were kids we used to hang out here a lot. Whenever one of us got in trouble, or just needed a place to hang for a while, cool off or think things over, this is where we came." A half smile lifted the corner of her generous mouth. "This became the safe haven. Stemmed from playing hide-and-seek here when we were kids. Remember when you were a kid and you'd run and play hide-and-seek, and you'd try your hardest to reach base before you got tagged?" she asked Sonia who nodded her head in agreement.

Although there were times when she traveled with her parents that Sonia had been in countries outside the United States, hide-and-seek seemed to be a universal game all kids knew and loved.

"It was one of my favorites," she replied in remembrance.

"Yeah. That was always one of my favorite games as a kid, too. This was where we all used to play the game. Somehow it's always been the place to draw me as an adult. My safe place." She turned around, her gaze encompassing the ranch as far as they could see.

"The Kealoha has been my safe haven. When my father retired, and I went to school, I always knew I would return to the ranch."

"Did you do so right away?" Sonia asked. "Come back to the ranch?" she clarified, and Ailani shook her head.

"Not at first. It took me a while to come back. Did a bit of traveling, finished working on my master's," she said, and must have caught Sonia's surprise as she laughed. "Does that surprise you that I have a master's degree and I'm a rancher?" she asked, one brow raised, hand on hip.

"No, not at all! Key has one, as does Nick," Sonia replied. "I just didn't realize you had, too. But it doesn't surprise me. The people, as well as this amazing ranch, stopped surprising me a long time ago," Sonia said, and the other woman grinned.

"Most people thought the reason I left was because of the relationship Nick and I once had. But it wasn't. I always knew I would return. No other place felt…right," she said, and for a moment Sonia envied her, the sense of home the other woman felt at the ranch.

Sonia had never felt like that about any place. She wondered if she ever would.

Ailani continued to speak, unaware of Sonia's disquiet. "I came back because here…I feel like I have a real home here. A real family. The Kealohas are really special folks. It was just my dad and I for a long time. I never really knew my mom. She died before I was old enough to even walk," she said with a shrug. "And the boys…their parents, always made us feel at home here. The fact that I was… different," she said, alluding to her dual heritage of African-American and Hawaiian, "didn't matter. Family is family, was what their parents always said." She paused, her glance taking in the horizon, hugging her arms around her waist as she gazed out over the west pasture where the rising sun was coming into view.

"That has now become a motto of sorts at the Ke-aloha," she said, and both women were silent for long moments before Ailani spoke again.

"It's the only place I've ever felt like that. I couldn't imagine living anywhere else. Couldn't imagine any place else feeling like home. Do you know what I mean, Sonia?"

Even though she smiled and nodded her head, Sonia *didn't* know the feeling. She never had experienced that feeling.

And deep down she knew she had always been searching for that feeling of home Ailani spoke of.

"Keanu is special, Sonia. He loves this ranch, family, and those he calls family mean more to him than anything or anyone. He would do anything to protect both. I would hate to see him hurt. He's a good man," she said, and even though she spoke softly, the words rang as a warning.

Sonia turned to face her. "I would never hurt the Kealoha Ranch…or Key. They both mean more to me than I can say. I know I've just been here, in his world, in your home," she said, acknowledging what the ranch meant for Ailani, "for a short while, but both Key and his ranch…his family, mean a lot to me." Sonia made the admission freely, and although she wanted to look away, to hide the vulnerability she felt must be showing in her eyes, she held the other woman's gaze.

Ailani must have seen whatever she was looking

for in Sonia's gaze. Her face softened, again, and a genuine smile graced her face.

She turned, as did Sonia, and together they watched the sun rise, bringing in the new day.

Chapter 17

Key walked inside Sonia's office trailer, closing and locking the door behind him. After the last time they were in the trailer together, he didn't want a repeat of the interruption.

His glance raked the small space, a grin on his face as he remembered what he and Sonia had done.

If he had his way, they'd be doing the same thing again, this time with a more satisfying ending, he thought.

Not that they hadn't made up for the interruption.

Over the past few weeks the pair had been inseparable, and although no one said anything directly to him about it, no one was in the dark about their relationship.

The only person who seemed to be sour about

it was her assistant, and for the life of him, Key couldn't understand what in hell he'd done to the woman to make her hate him so.

He searched Sonia out and found her inside the smaller cubicle in the trailer that served as her office.

She was on the phone, the small tortoiseshell-framed glasses perched on the end of her pert nose, so absorbed in her work she hadn't heard him enter and didn't know he was in her trailer. She spun around at her desk, turning her back to him, and stood, staring out of the small window, pulling at a curl at the back of her head, a sign he knew that meant she was thinking, hard.

"Well, with the new angle, I think it'll be even more exciting!" she exclaimed, and he grinned at her enthusiasm.

"Awesome! I'll put it together for you and send it to you. I think the new angle will produce results you'll be pleased with."

He paused, leaning against the door frame, arms folded across his chest as he waited and listened.

He didn't in the least find that intimidating or off-putting. Her focus was one of the things he loved about her.

As soon as he thought it, he paused, his footsteps coming to a halt before he could walk toward her office.

He was falling for her, hard.

The feeling he got simply from looking at her mocked his earlier belief that it was only sex. It was more than just sex between them. Yeah, the sex was off the chain, incomparable. She did things to and for him no other woman could, but it was so much more.

He leaned against the door frame, the grin on his face still in place.

"Now back to work." Sonia sighed, disconnecting the call from one of her friends currently working on a project that Sonia was helping her to develop. Dee Dee had been given the project after a failed pilot. The network hadn't wanted to give the series another shot but, after revamping it, the show was given a new chance. Sonia had confidence that her friend could produce the results needed to see the show become a hit. She smiled, grateful to be in a position to help those few people she truly called friends.

She and Dee Dee had gone to film school together, and she knew her friend's work ethic matched her own. Lately an idea had been forming in the back of Sonia's mind as she contemplated another project with her friend and taking a stab at script writing for film. She shelved the thought as it was time to get back to work.

She spun around and returned to the document she'd been working on before her friend's interruption.

Back to her own show.

She smiled hugely. Now that she had Key and his family's approval—and signatures—on the dotted line, so to speak, the show could go on. She was beyond happy.

Everything was flowing right in her life, and she'd never been happier. The show was a success and, with the projections of the ratings, would be an even greater success for the upcoming season. And with the upcoming show she'd agreed to produce, her career was doing better than she could ever have imagined.

With the new show, she had been given full rein, and would relocate to Hawaii temporarily, flying out to L.A. when needed. And she had a man in her life she was absolutely crazy about.

Or cray cray, as Dee Dee would say, she thought, her friend's earlier description of her feelings for Keanu.

She giggled out loud, shrugging. The fact that she had entertained the idea of staying in Hawaii to produce both shows was her own self-indicator that she was committed to Key, enough to see if what they had was special, and something that could be more long-term.

Before, the thought of that would have sent her running for the hills. The smile on her face blossomed.

Not anymore.

Sonia was so busy at her desk, keying into the document the upcoming film schedule, that it took a long time before she realized she wasn't alone.

"Could life get any better?" she asked, and jumped in her chair when she got an answer.

"I think I know the answer to that."

The deep familiar baritone had her startled gaze flying to the source.

"Hey, baby, I didn't see you there! How'd you sneak up on me?" she asked, laughing at their inner joke. They both had come to the conclusion that they must have inner radar going on between them as each time one was within a foot of the other, they immediately knew.

Key walked up to her and she rose, a grin in place as he approached.

"Hmm," he answered, nuzzling the side of her neck, placing a string of hot, searing little kisses along her skin that raised a rash of goose bumps down her back. She arched into his embrace. "Guess I better up my game if you no longer are…affected, by my presence," he murmured, grinding softly against her.

"Hmm, no need for that. You affect me plenty enough," she replied, her eyes closed, enjoying the feel of her man against her. She pulled away from him, frowning, remembering his statement moments before his short but deadly kisses robbed her of co-herent thought.

"Hey, wait a minute…what would be the answer?" she asked, and released a surprised yelp when he lifted her up, placed his big palms beneath her butt and plopped her down on the desk.

"The question to if life could get any better. If you come away with me for the weekend, I can guarantee you the answer to that would be a firm yes," he said. "Just you and me, baby. No interruptions."

Immediately he bumped her legs apart and settled between her thighs. The grin on her face grew and she wrapped her arms around his neck.

She tilted her head to the side so she could see him fully, placing what she knew he *had* to know was a feigned look of disbelief on her face, all the while trying as hard as she could to keep the grin from breaking free. She raised a brow.

"Oh, yeah, just me and you? No farm duties to take you away from me this time?"

Key removed her glasses from her face and placed them, rim up, on the desk.

He kissed the top of her nose. "Have I told you how damn sexy you are in those, by the way?" he asked, nodding toward her glasses, his deep voice sending shivers over her body.

"Hmm…you might have mentioned it, once or twice," she quipped. He brought his head down low, kissed her, grabbing the bottom rim of her lip and tugging it into his mouth, slowly allowing it to pop back out.

"So damn sexy," he replied, his voice catching.

"Hmm," she murmured softly. Her smile could no longer be kept away, coming out as she gave her approval of his kisses.

When she glanced up at him, she caught the look

in his eyes and felt her heart respond in kind, the beat thumping stronger, harder against her chest. For a moment they simply stared at each other, neither one able or wanting to look away.

She loved him.

Oh, God, she loved him.

The minute the thought entered her mind, she shied away from it, burying the feeling away to study later.

It was less than a minute, their examination of the other, but the effect left her shaky. She knew that whatever had passed between them, she hadn't been alone in how it made her feel. She brought her hand up, caressed the strong line of his jaw.

Stubborn jaw for a stubborn man.

But not just any stubborn man. He was her stubborn man. The grin blossomed.

He brought his hand up to the back of her head, tunneled his fingers within the strands and brought their heads close enough so that their foreheads touched, saying nothing. No words were needed.

The moment went from intimate to something *more*.

He continued, clearing his throat. "In answer to your question, nope. Just the two of us, as the old song goes," he said, and bent to kiss her again, as though he couldn't help it. "No ranch chores. No crazy fan hitting me with water." He kept speaking even as she burst out laughing, remembering the incident he referred to when they'd been on a date in town and a tourist had recognized Key. In her...excitement to meet him she'd tripped and the glass of water she'd held had drenched Key.

He'd surprised Sonia by his tolerance and the way he'd smiled at the woman and given her an autograph, seeking to ease her embarrassment. She knew how it pained him to be recognized in the first place and to sign an autograph really took him out of his comfort zone. But for the elderly woman he'd done both.

"No old woman asking if I would like to meet her daughter, that we would make pretty babies together," he continued, his sensual mouth quirking in the corner in response to her giggles. He kissed her softly, and she sighed into his mouth, her hands tightening around his neck.

"You know, I thought you had set that up," she said, chuckling out loud at the horrified look on his face.

"Why would you think that?"

"I don't know, it was all so over-the-top!" she replied around her chuckles. "I mean, I know you're fine and everything—to me, that is—but really, that was carrying it too far!" She giggled outright at his expression.

"Fine, huh? You think I'm that good-looking?" he asked, and she groaned.

"As if you didn't know," she scoffed, but the smile remained. For as handsome as he was, and the amount of wealth he had, she knew Key could have taken far more advantage of both of those facts than he did.

Saying that, she also knew her man was no saint, as was made evident by the second event of that evening, the woman who tried to throw water on him.

"Yeah, well, I'd say you take full press advantage of that. Case in point, water in face? Need I remind you?" she quipped. She could do no less than to bring that to his attention. It was her duty, as his woman.

"God, I won't ever live that down, will I?" Key belted out a snort before groaning at the memory. He caught her hands within his, bringing them back to his chest, kissing her fist. "Besides, that wasn't me that woman wanted. It was all Nick's fault!" He blamed his twin and she gave him the side eye.

"Yeah, well, I'll guess I'll let you off the hook about that one," she conceded eventually. The woman had mistaken him for his brother, after all, as she called him Nicky, babbling in her hysteria.

Teasing Key had become the highlight of her night. Besides, she loved to see him smile, and his laugh was one that brought an answering smile to her own mouth.

Less than a month ago, there was no way anyone could have told her that she and Key would not only be seeing one another but that they would be immensely enjoying their time together.

The glowing ember of love that was growing inside her, for him, was intensifying. She had been the one to bring out the unbridled passion in him.

"That's one of the things I love about you," he said, and when he bent to kiss her this time, not only was she unable to respond from sheer shock, she barely kept herself from falling off the desk at his words.

She swallowed and turned her face up to him, trying to hide the surprise she felt at the wording. Obviously he hadn't realized what he'd said; she knew from his facial expression, the soft smile still in place, that he hadn't.

"Oh, yeah?" she asked in response once he released her lips. "What's that?"

"You have never mistaken me for my twin," he said, and although he made the quip lightly, she knew that it held significance for him.

She opened her mouth for a quick comeback but instead closed it.

The comeback kid, as he once called her, referring to her quick wit, had nothing to say.

"Nick can handle anything that comes up," he said, going back to the subject, and brought her body closer to his, nudging against her.

"Ooh, are you sure about that?" she said when she felt his hard cock bump against the center of her jeans as she ground softly against his hardness. She couldn't resist the quip or smirk. It was who she was. She choked back a laugh.

He lifted her high, cutting off her laugh midgiggle, and brought her body down the length of his so she could feel every hard inch of him.

"Don't even joke like that. You're all mine," he replied, and took her lips with his.

She sighed, giving in to the kiss. Despite his tendency to be slightly...possessive of her, she couldn't help but be turned on by the way he gave her all of his...attention.

He placed two big palms on either side of her cheeks, his mouth opening to deepen the kiss. When she felt his tongue lap against the seam of her lips, she willingly gave in to his demand for entry.

The kiss was hot, sweet yet hard. Hands that framed her face slid down, past her shoulders and waist to cup her backside in each hard, capable hand. When he squeezed each butt cheek and pressed her closer, she groaned into his openmouthed kiss.

Just like that, he had her up in flames. He took her to places no man ever had. Although she had never made love before him, she'd been a sexual person, stopping just shy of actual penetration, so it wasn't as if she was...new to the act of lovemaking.

As he kissed and plundered her lips, his hands loosened the scrunchie from her hair, drawing it away and tossing it to the desk behind her, allowing her curly hair to land on her back and shoulders.

When she felt him tunnel his hands into her hair, she moaned, moving closer. She knew how much he loved her hair, the feel of it against his hands.

Slowly he drew away from her, one hand remaining in the nest of her hair, the other moving up her body to hold on to her waist, steadying her.

And it was a good thing he did.

Had he not held on to her she would have fallen down on her face when he released her.

He smiled. Sonia blushed.

Arrogant man. He knew how he affected her.

"Liked that, did you?" he asked, his rich, sexy voice deep...and all full of himself. His masculine satisfaction was so large she wondered how they all fit, him, his ego and her, in the small room.

Sonia kept the grin from her face, barely. What was good for the goose and all that....

She tugged her bottom lip, allowing her loosened hair to fall into her eyes slightly. She knew how it turned him on whenever she did that.

She stopped at his belt buckle, toyed with it a bit before allowing her fingers to slip down even farther to brush over the evidence of her effect on him.

She felt it jump against her fingers. Her delight grew, yet she kept her face down so he wouldn't see her. When she lightly cupped him in the palm of her hand, the grin on her face broke free at his deep, indrawn breath.

"Yeah...about as much as you did, Key," she said, her voice low. "I mean, you did enjoy it, didn't you?" she asked.

She chose that moment to glance up at him as she unzipped his jeans and deftly slipped a hand inside.

"Baby..."

Chapter 18

His harsh groan bounced off the walls when she brushed her fingers across the top of his phallus before pulling it out.

"What are you doing, woman?" His grumble was low, guttural.

"Whatever you want me to do to you," she answered. When she unzipped his jeans, slowly peeling the fly away so she could completely lift him out, she leaned down and softly placed a kiss on the soft skin covering his shaft.

At that moment, Key had never been so glad to have had the foresight to lock a door.

Slowly she withdrew his shaft, a smile playing around the corners of her lips as she saw how hard he'd grown for her.

"Is this all for me?" she asked, and grinned hugely when he groaned.

Running the tip of her finger over the soft slit at the center of his shaft, she smiled. "Yeah, I think it is," she said, and he allowed her to play with him for a few moments longer before he could take no more of her teasing.

"Time to pay the piper, little girl," he said roughly, and deftly unzipped her jeans, shoved them down the length of her legs, panties and all, and kicked them to the side.

"Key!" she exclaimed. When he lifted her by the bottom and walked over to her chair with her, she tumbled into his lap.

She placed her palms over each side of his face, her gaze intent on his. "It's a price I'll gladly pay," she said softly.

His attention became riveted on her small tongue as it darted out and moistened her full, lush lips.

"Oh, yeah?" he asked, his voice coming out as little more than a growl.

"Yeah…why don't you let me show you?" Without another word she raised her body and slowly lowered herself onto his rock-hard shaft.

His groan mimicked her slow drawn-out moan as she slowly began to ride him.

"Baby, we can't keep going like this…we don't have protection," he said, and her eyes widened. In all the time they'd made love, even though she was on the pill, they'd always used a condom.

She moaned, her head dropping onto her chest.

"Don't worry, I'll take care of you, baby," he said, and, holding on to her waist, he lifted her up and away, the slow hiss of their bodies disengaging with a soft *pop*.

Sonia watched with hooded eyes as he lifted her and placed her on the desk in front of him, stood and fumbled for his wallet in the jeans he still wore.

He grinned at her when he produced the desired object, showing her the little foiled square protection.

She didn't know whether to be happy or angry that he so readily had a condom.

"Before you, I didn't keep them at the ready. But I never know when you're going to attack me, hungry beast that you are," he replied, reading her unspoken words.

He pulled his jeans down far enough this time so that his cock sprang completely free.

"Hmm," Sonia said as soon as his glorious shaft was revealed.

"Like what you see?" he asked with a grunt as he rolled the condom over his cock. He grinned at her and sat back in the chair, plopping her back down in his lap as he did so.

Before she could make a rebuttal, he lifted her and eased her back down on his shaft.

As soon as she was fully seated, she widened her legs, allowing them to drop over his thighs as she slowly began to ride him.

In the position she was in, she couldn't see his face, which made it feel somehow forbidden…erotic.

When he palmed the undersides of her breasts, his thumbs brushing over her hardened nipples, she bit the side of her cheek to prevent the cries from erupting. At three in the afternoon, anyone could walk by and hear them, a thought that had her struggling to keep quiet as he worked his magic, his depth of stroke hitting her spot with delicious precision, his fingers bringing magic to both her clitoris and breasts in hot synchronicity.

She felt her orgasm hovering and, wanting to bring him over the edge with her, she raised her bottom enough so that she could slip a hand between them and lightly grasp his sac. His low growl was her reward.

Nearly lifting her in midair, he brought his hands around her waist and stroked quickly into her, over and over, his thrusts becoming short, swift, deadly, until with one final stroke together they went over the edge.

It took long moments for her world to calm and her heartbeat to slow to a regulated beat. She blew out a long breath, her body limp.

As she'd been coming down from the high of her orgasm, Key had lifted her and turned her around so that she lay, slumped, against his chest.

Once her breath had calmed, she opened one eye to find him staring at her.

"You're incredible, do you know that?" he asked, and she grinned.

"I think you're pretty incredible, too," she quipped, in an attempt to keep it light. Each time they made love, she felt that much closer to Key. Every day she spent with him, the thought of how she would leave, once the time came, was harder to face.

Despite her every intention, she'd fallen in love with him. She felt tears spring to her eyes and, unable to stand it, she rose and, with a shaky smile, tears falling from her face, she grabbed her discarded jeans and ran from the room, heading toward the small bathroom in the trailer, needing a moment to get herself together.

Alone inside the bathroom, she splashed water on her face and took deep breaths.

She had to tell him. Had to let him know how she felt, how much she loved him. After speaking with Dee, a plan had been forming in the back of her mind, a plan where she could spend more time in Hawaii. More time with him.

She didn't want what they had to be over until they'd had a chance…he'd had a chance, to love her as desperately as she loved him.

She knew he cared about her—even though he'd never said the actual words, she knew he did. The type of connection they had was rare, and she had no intention on letting it—or him—go.

She smiled shakily as she turned the knob to leave the room, knowing what she wanted and, most important, no longer afraid to reach out for it.

Chapter 19

"Is that how you got so far at such a young age?" The words were hurled at her the moment she stepped back into the room.

"What are you talking about?" she asked, cautiously walking toward Key, who stood near her oversize messenger bag. When she walked closer, she saw that he held a several pieces of paper in his hand, bound by a clip. The hand that held the paperwork shook.

"Key...baby, are you okay?" she asked walking closer.

"Was it the guilt that brought the tears? Is that why you just ran out of the room? Or do you have aspirations of leaving producing and becoming an actress? Which one is it?" His angry words were hurled at her like darts, each one piercing, direct.

"Key, I don't understand, why—" Her question dangled midsentence when he handed her the sheaf of paperwork.

Surprised, she saw that it was the contract she'd recently gotten back from legal, the one they'd drafted after Key and his family had given their final approval. All documents had signatures—his and his brother's and father's and hers.

The only problem was that it wasn't the contract she'd given him.

Her face lost all color as she read the contents. She glanced from him to the paperwork, dumbfounded. "I don't understand any of this. Who... What?" She shook her head and felt her heart sink at the look on his face as he stared at her, one side of his lip curled.

"You and all the rest of you won't get away with this bullshit. I'll fight you in court. I didn't sign that contract. I don't know how you did it...why you did it, but we won't let you get away with this."

"Key, you have to know that I had nothing to do with this! I would never lie to your family and create something like this. I don't even know what this is all about."

"Oh, please, give it a damn rest, Sonia. I don't know how you found out the details about our family, but you won't get to blast my family's business for the entire world to know. I'll see your ass in court before you do," he said, the anger in his face and voice making her heart break, and tears of anger and confusion run down her face, unchecked.

Sonia was thunderstruck, not only by his words but what the contract read. In the contract was an amendment stating the Kealohas were giving the production company full approval to contact a family by the name of Wilde, who owned a ranch in Wyoming that was run by the foster sons of Jedediah Clint Wilde.

The biological father of Keanu and Nick Kealoha.

"So…is that how you did it?" He threw the words at her, his back to her as he stood at the door to her trailer. "Made it to the top? By screwing your way there?" His bark of laughter was harsh and without humor.

She slowly turned around to face him.

"Really? Are you honestly accusing me of what I think you are? You think I would do something like this? I don't know how…or why this happened. But…you believe I did it. Dear God, man, your idiocy is bigger than Mauna Loa!" She named the active volcano on the big island as she hurled the insult, her voice high, not caring who may come by and hear her.

Red stole across the lower line of his stubborn jaw, his face tightening with anger.

He opened his mouth to speak and she held up a palm. "Don't. Don't say another word. Because if you do, I will be *bound* by the oath I took, the creed I stand by, to retort. And what I say won't be…nice," she replied. She saw the look on his face, a look of curiosity mixed with anger.

"What damn creed?" he yelled, his booming voice echoing off the trailer walls.

"The 'don't curse out a damn fool who questions my ethics' creed. That's what creed!" she yelled back, her voice louder, more strident than his. She took a deep breath, narrowed her eyes.

"And you are the biggest asshat who has *ever* made tempted me to break my creed," she angrily spit, with only a small catch in her voice to belie the true sense of betrayal she felt.

She was proud of herself that she was able to hold it together.

But she knew she had to get the hell out of there, because if she didn't there was no telling what she would say to him. Or do.

Her gaze angrily scanned him, head to toe, her eyes landing briefly on the rope near his feet. Images came to mind instantly of what she'd like to do with that rope. And she could promise one thing—it damn well wouldn't be sexy.

"I am *done* with *you*," she began, and pointed a finger at him. "If you think I'm capable of something so…so heinous, then you don't know me. You never have." The last words were torn from her throat as she rushed from the trailer, not wanting him to see the tears of anger, betrayal and love rolling down her face. "And you have no need to haul my ass in court, because I'll make sure that whoever…however this happened, your family won't suffer from it. Unlike you, I know a little something about loyalty." She said the final words, her voice breaking. "Now get out."

"Sonia!" She heard him bellow but didn't turn around to look at him.

"Go!" she hurled, unable to take any more. Pain of betrayal was tearing her apart. She didn't know if she could ever forgive him for thinking she'd hurt him in such a callous way.

Alone in her hotel room less than an hour later, Sonia haphazardly grabbed clothes. Fisting them, she stuffed them into her suitcase with tears streaming, unchecked, down her face.

After Key had left, she'd rushed around the trailer and hurriedly packed her belongings, including the damning contract. On her way to her car she'd brushed past Nick, nearly knocking him over.

"Hey, whoa there, where's the fire, Sonia?" Nick's deep voice, so similar to Key's, brought another fresh wave of tears to scorch down the line of her cheeks.

She couldn't bear to look into the face of someone who looked so much like the man she both loved and now hated. A man who would think she could betray him and his family so easily. She clenched her teeth to force the bitter anger and resentful tears away.

Nodding her head toward the stable, she said, "Go ask your brother. I'm sure he will more than oblige you with all the gory details. No fears, I'll be out of here as soon as I can get the next plane to the mainland!"

"What the hell—" The rest of his words were said to her retreating back as Sonia literally ran away, her boots kicking up dust as she sprinted toward her car.

As her tires pealed out of the long driveway and she sped away, Sonia allowed the tears to fall even as she tried, frantically, to think.

She knew that she had nothing to prove. She hadn't been involved in the betrayal, hadn't been the one expose his secret, his family's secret. She had been just as surprised, as hurt, as Key. She had nothing on her side but the fact that she loved him.

Evidently it wasn't enough.

She straightened her back, firmed her quivering bottom lip. She had two objectives, and the first was to find out how this had happened.

By the time she got back to her hotel, one of those questions was answered. When she checked the front desk, she found that her assistant had checked out earlier that day.

And she'd had the nerve to leave her a note detailing exactly how she felt about Sonia. Although she hadn't admitted to what she'd done, she'd left Sonia no doubt that she was responsible for what had happened.

How could she have been so blind? How could she have not seen how Patricia really felt about her?

Numb, she'd read the note, tears slipping down her face, nausea welling, again, in her gut.

She'd felt as though she'd been broadsided by a Mack truck.

In one day she had lost it all. Her reputation, her assistant and her man.

The nausea threatened to overcome her.

Chapter 20

Key sightlessly read the newspaper, his eyes scanning the printed words without seeing them. In between times spent worrying about his father and his brother, his thoughts were, as they had been for nearly two weeks, on Sonia.

Unbelievable, the things he'd said to her still echoed in his mind.

Self-loathing was his new best friend.

He knew she had nothing to do with the betrayal, knew it with everything inside of him, yet he'd called her names he knew she would never forgive him for. All because he was afraid of the feelings she stirred in him.

"So, why don't you go tell her that you love her?

And that you're an ass. Don't forget that part. Women love when we admit that."

His father's tired voice made Key jump and he stared over at him lying in the bed.

"Hey, Dad, how you feeling?" he asked, walking toward his father's bedside. "Do you need anything?"

Alek Kealoha's dark brown eyes stared up into Key's so long he grew uncomfortable beneath the piercing gaze.

His father sighed, his shoulders slumping, and Key found himself really looking at the man he'd called father for his entire life.

Like Key and Nick, Alek Kealoha was tall, nearly equal in height to Key's six feet four inches, but time had narrowed his once-broad shoulders and grayed his once-dark brown hair.

"No one but my eldest would make a fool of himself and ruin the best thing that has ever happened to him."

Key sighed and looked away. "Dad, I don't want to talk 'bout it. Just leave it alone." Key had known that Alek was aware of what had happened; he'd known that Nick had told his father what transpired between him and Sonia.

"No, son, I'm not going to leave it alone," Alek said, his voice strengthening.

At that moment Nick walked into his room, his bright blue eyes darting between Key and their father.

Slowly he walked over to one of the free chairs

and, flipping it around, straddled the seat. He didn't need to say a word. The tension in the room was palpable.

Yet he did.

"What's up? Are we finally gonna talk all this out?" he asked, and although his expression remained light, Key knew his brother was feeling anything *but* calm.

"Yes, son," Alek began, giving his attention to Nick. "We have quite a few things to talk about. And we will. But first things first." Alek turned away from Nick to face Key. "Key...look, don't make the same mistake I made with your mother."

Key felt an immediate denial, not wanting to hear, not wanting to *know* what happened between his parents, but understanding that his father needed to share it with him. He glanced over at his twin.

Although his expression remained calm, the tic in his cheek told Key that his brother's mind was set. Key knew that his father wanted...needed to unload his burden.

"Okay, Dad. We're listening," he finally said, including his brother as he steeled himself for whatever his father had to say.

"Your mother and I loved each other from the time we were kids. We had the kind of love that the elders didn't even call puppy love. Everyone knew it. We knew it. It was real. But I was stupid. I didn't trust that our love was real and I accused your mother of cheating on me. I didn't give her time to explain, and in my anger I went out and did what I thought she had done to me," he said, and Key hid his reaction, the surprise at what his father was disclosing.

"When I found out the truth, that it was one of the stable hands trying to break us apart by spreading lies, it was too late. The damage had been done and your mother left the Island." He turned away, his voice cracking.

He went on to tell them how their mother left for California to stay with family, that the only way he'd heard from her had been though her parents. Although they knew he'd hurt their only daughter, they also knew he loved her and deeply regretted what he'd done.

Eventually he convinced her parents to tell him where he could find her and had gone after her.

"It took a lot of pleading, begging, but she took me back. My A'Kela took me back," he said, and Key felt the unexpected tears of emotion burn his eyes as he listened to his father, watched the sadness and then happiness burn in his dark brown eyes.

"We didn't know she was pregnant until after we were married. We got married as soon as we got back home. She told me she'd...met a man while she was there and they'd had a relationship. But she didn't want to stay with him. She suspected she was pregnant but didn't tell him. She said he was a good man, but he wasn't ready to be a father." The smile he gave to Key and Nick was a bittersweet one.

"I knew your mother was pregnant, but that didn't

matter. I begged her to marry me and she said yes. And from that moment on, you boys were my sons. We never told you about your...father, because there was no need. I was—am—your father," he said, tears falling down his aged cheeks.

By the time he'd finished, both Nick and Key were at their father's side, embracing him.

When they broke away his father's dark eyes held Key's light blue ones.

"Don't be an ass like your old man. Go after your woman, son, before it's too late," he said, and Key and Nick both laughed and exchanged looks over his head.

He was back to his succinct way of speech.

Their father was going to be okay.

Chapter 21

Beyond exhausted, bordering on sleep deprivation that was compounded by jet lag stemming from her back-to-back trips from L.A. to New Jersey, Sonia let herself into the guesthouse Nick had allowed her to stay in.

During the past week, she'd managed not only to save her job but also convince both Marty and Sheldon, her executive producers, to allow her to speak to the Kealohas. Not in an attempt to convince them to allow a second season—she knew that was out of the question—but to prevent the Kealohas from "hauling their collective asses to court," as Marty so succinctly put it.

No way in hell she wanted that to happen. Her ass,

or *any* part of her, going to court facing a lawsuit for breach of contract was not an option, now or ever.

Thankfully the men had enough pull that one word from them to *Global Media,* the publication Patricia was in league with, pulled the plug on any leakage of the private information about the Kealohas and the Wildes.

"Damn you, Patricia," she cursed. Even to think of her former assistant brought a fresh wave of anger.

Damn woman was lucky Sonia didn't run up on her and deliver a dose of civilian justice.

She laughed at her own foolishness at the notion. She'd been watching way too many gangster movies lately, as well.

And, of course, thinking of her love for gangster movies brought a sad smile to her face as she remembered the late-night date she and Key had shared after work when she'd giggled, confiding her love of all things gangster. He'd promptly opened his media chest, a pirate's cove of treasures; every gangster movie from *Scarface* to *Pulp Fiction* was within its hallowed depths.

They'd spent the next hours in bed, eyes glued to the mounted flat screen in his bedroom as she lay against his chest in his big king-size bed, a bowl of popcorn stationed on the bedside table.

After she'd found and confronted Patricia all she'd felt for her was pity. Sonia knew that any opportunity she thought she'd had or would gain was all for naught. Although business to the bone, Marty and Sheldon were two men whom one did not mess with.

Something Patricia had learned the hard way.

During their long association, no matter what doubts she'd had about Patricia, Sonia would have never thought the woman could be so cold-blooded. That she could stab her in the back the way she'd done. Sonia had learned that her assistant, beneath the warm smiles and hugs, was a ruthless woman who would do whatever it took to get what she wanted. Apparently she thought the way back to the top, the way to revive her career, was by destroying Sonia's. She'd been so twisted with jealousy she'd been willing to betray and hurt Sonia.

How had she ever been so stupid that she hadn't seen through her guise? Sonia wondered, pain at the betrayal still lingering.

She knew that she would never know that answer. In the end, it didn't matter. It stung, hurt like hell actually, but she would survive. What she wondered was if she could survive what it had done to her relationship with Key, the first man she'd ever given herself to, the first man she'd ever loved.

His image the last time she'd seen him, face tight with anger, blue eyes swirling with emotions ranging from hurt...to love, to anger, slipped past her defenses and into her mind.

"Oh, God." The raw pain and whispered words were torn from her throat. She swallowed down the tears.

Now, all she wanted to do was curl up in the fetal position and go to sleep for the next twenty-four hours. And, thanks to Nick, that's exactly what she planned to do, as her meeting with him and his father wasn't scheduled until tomorrow.

When Nick had contacted her she'd been at first suspicious of his call, knowing that Key must have told him what had gone down.

Nick had said that not only had Key told them what happened, but their father had suffered a mild stroke after hearing the story.

The guilt alone nearly broke her down.

Nick had gently told her that although his father had what the doctors called a "mini stroke," he was fine and recovering in the hospital.

She knew it was yet another reason for Key to hate her.

She'd explained to Nick what happened, with a promise that none of the information would ever be indulged. To that end, she had a document, signed and dated with her name, and Marty's and Sheldon's, stating that fact. She wanted to send it via carrier to them but knew that she owed them a face-to-face visit. It was the least she could do.

He'd been silent and carefully listened to her. And although she wondered if he believed her, after he had invited her to come to the ranch and talk to him and his father, promising her that Key was away buying new livestock, she'd accepted the invitation.

It was the height of tourist season, he'd told her,

and he doubted at such short notice she'd be able to secure a room. When he'd offered her the guest cottage she'd gladly accepted.

She glanced down at her watch, frowning as she checked the time. It was barely nine in the morning. With the time difference between Hawaii and L.A. she figured that she would be able to grab some shuteye and not look like death warmed over before her meeting with the men the next day.

She dragged her small suitcase inside the room and sagged against the closed door for a moment before she groped for a light switch and flicked on the lights. Although she was beyond beat, she took in the room with great appreciation. Simply furnished, beautiful.

The small guesthouse was mostly taken up by the large room, the bed on a platform on one side of the room, flanked by a complete wall of windows overlooking the west side of the ranch. It felt like…home.

A tired, bittersweet smile lifted the corner of her mouth as she left her suitcase abandoned at the front door. She walked over to the small sofa in front of the bed and sank down on the soft cushions. She knew she had better get up; if not, she'd fall dead asleep right where she was.

She kicked off her shoes and, yawning hugely, she arched her back before sagging against the back of the sofa briefly, mind and body both exhausted.

Sighing, she quickly divested herself of her clothing and stood. Wearing nothing but her panties, she padded over to the bed and drew back the colorful spread.

A grin of appreciation settled across her face when her nearly naked body met the cool, soft, high-quality sheets. As she nestled into the sheets, the image of Key's face the last time she saw him drifted across her mind.

She didn't know if she should be happy or sad that he wasn't going to be around when she spoke with Nick and his father tomorrow. One part of her knew it was the right thing to do. After their last angry exchange, she knew that if, and when, the time came that he wanted to speak to her, it would have to be him taking the initiative. There was no way on God's green earth he would want anything to do with her.

The bitter anger and betrayal she felt ran deep. But, for as badly as she hurt, that Key would believe her capable of something so awful, a part of her understood his pain. More than anything she hated that she had been the one to cause his family so much grief, beyond the show. The fact that his father had been okay, medically, had done little to alleviate the mountainous amount of guilt she felt that one of her staff members had been responsible for the attack.

No wonder the man hated her. She sighed, nestling her body farther down into the covers. She was lucky Nick and his father had agreed to see her. When she'd received the call from them, she'd been not only surprised, but also very grateful.

Now she would do everything she could to make

it up to Key to his family. That was the least she could do. As far as Key was concerned…she drew in a breath, blowing it out in a small gush of air. There wasn't a lot she could do about that. It was up to him.

Tears slipped down her face as she allowed her body and mind to relax, and she succumbed to mindless exhaustion.

Keanu raised his key to place in the lock, surprised when the knob turned without assistance. He frowned, before shrugging it off. Although the guest cottage was rarely used, and those who worked the ranch were trusted, after their mother had passed away, they'd kept the doors locked.

Oh, well. He'd ask Ailani about it when he saw her next.

Once inside, he groped blindly for the light switch but changed his mind. He knew the cabin like the back of his hand, and he was just going to fall into bed, anyway.

He slipped off his shoes and eased his jeans down the length of his legs, kicking them away. He grabbed his ends of his T-shirt and lifted it over his head before padding over to where the bed was. Once there, he sat down at the foot and yanked off socks.

He was so damn tired, all he wanted to do was lay down and sleep until Monday.

After being gone for the past week, he had no more perspective on the situation than he'd had the day he left.

It had been a tense month, but as soon as his father had been cleared from the hospital, and Keanu was assured he was going to be okay, he'd left the ranch. He'd needed time away to clear his head.

His plan had been to stay away for the next two weeks, but when his brother had called to tell him he needed to return to oversee the renovations on the house, he'd grudgingly agreed to do it.

The house had been locked up when he'd returned, and not up to dealing with a bunch of workmen's mess, he'd opted, at his brother's suggestion, to use the guest cottage.

Although he wasn't in the mood for questions—or advice—from anyone in the family, he'd come home once Nick told him he and his father planned to stay in a hotel near the house for a few days, as the dust and smoke was bothering his father.

For that reason and that reason alone, Key had agreed to come home, sending his foreman to finish the job of purchasing equipment.

He loved his family, but he still needed time to think without anyone offering their opinion. It was probably too late with Sonia, anyway, he thought, sighing. The talk with her parents hadn't exactly been…forthcoming.

"Damn," he muttered, "I've screwed this all up." His face tightened as he drew in a deep breath, standing to stretch. He'd game-plan it all tomorrow. Right now he needed sleep.

He padded, naked, to the bed and lifted the down comforter and slipped inside, sleep claiming him as soon as his head hit the pillow.

Chapter 22

The dream came softly, slowly, blowing into her mind as a lover slipped into a bed. A hard, warm arm was thrown across her breast, callused fingers toying with her nipples, one big thigh clamped over both of hers as his cock speared gently between her buttocks.

She moaned in pleasure, settling back against the even harder body attached to the arm and leg. And cock.

"Hmm," she murmured, allowing the dream to continue, not wanting it to ever end.

With a soft sigh and lazy smile on her face, she allowed herself to drift into the sensations, taking each one in, glorying in the feel of hot, hard masculinity blanketing her body.

* * *

The dream dragged into his mind, bringing his cock to rock-hard awareness even as he slept. A woman, soft, warm, was nestled tight against his body, her sweet soft ass nestling his hardening shaft. He grasped one plump breast and thumbed it, feeling it spike against his hand in gratitude.

A throaty moan was his reward and Key brought her closer, his hand moving from one plump breast to travel down the line of her chest, past her slightly rounded tummy to tangle and nest in her soft thatch of curls, slipping his fingers inside the elastic band of her panties.

Inserting a thick finger deep inside her heat, he twirled it around and groaned when he felt her body's response, as her walls clamped down on the single digit, tugging it, begging for more.

Desire drew an answer from his own body; his shaft hardened to granite and poked against her sweet backside, demanding attention. When she lifted up and ground on it, he felt his face tighten.

The dream was as hot as it got. He wanted nothing more than to shift that sweet little body of hers beneath him and lose himself inside her heat, her warmth.

But he wanted it to last. Even as he dreamed, he knew he wanted it to last. He knew that when he awoke, the dream would be over. If he couldn't make it last with her in real life, he damn well would hold on to what he could in the dream.

Slowly, he withdrew his fingers from her body, satisfied when she cried out in protest.

Just as she always did.

The truth of that struck him hard, nagging at him, but he allowed the dream to unfold.

Her soft mewling cries were his undoing.

He flipped her body over and covered it with his, taking her mouth in one long, drugging kiss as he ground his body into hers.

"Hmm," his lover moaned into his open mouth. The satisfaction he felt from the pleasure he was giving her again gave him pause.

Her pleasure came before his. It always had. It always would....

He remained silent. He would give her everything he had, if only in dream. He would show her what she meant to him. Give of himself without holding back.

He found her heat and stroked inside, giving it to her in the way he knew she had come to love, his fingers delving deep inside, grinding softly into her sweet pussy while his thumb toyed with her tight blood-filled clit.

His cock was so hard it was nearly painful, as lust and desire for her beat down on him, nearly driving him past his control. But he wanted...needed to give more.

He pulled his mouth from hers and traced her lips with his tongue.

"I love you, Key...please make love to me," she whispered.

And that was all it took.

All it took to drag Key's eyes open, force him to shake the embers of sleep away. This was real—she was real. He'd missed her....

As he stared down at her, he didn't question why she was in his bed, didn't question why she was locked in a dream, why she was so tired she didn't lift her eyes and look at him. She was in the dreamy in-between state, just as he had been.

God, how he'd missed this woman. He'd been... lost without her. The admission didn't make him angry, didn't make him go running out to the woods, as she'd accused him, afraid of his emotions, afraid to admit how he felt.

He stared down at her. It was time he admitted how he felt about her...how she made him feel. To show her that he trusted her with his life.

The grin grew wolfish. And time to give her something to really dream about.

He peeled the sheet down, away from her, exposing her body to his hungry stare.

The moonlight beaming down through the skylight gleamed on her pretty brown body, her plump breasts arched, her nipples tight...begging for his touch.

He could do nothing but oblige.

He lowered his head and swiped his tongue out across the crest of first one breast, then the other, before pulling one thickened nub deep into his mouth. Simultaneously, he lowered one hand to lift her butt, and the other slid down between their close bodies to find her center.

He toyed with it. Played with and teased it…made her squirm around his fingers.

Before ripping her panties away from her body.

"Oh…mmm…" Her strangled, garbled moan brought him satisfaction. But it wasn't enough. He needed to give her more. He needed more from her.

He pulled away from her spot despite her protests, while he withdrew his fingers from her clenching heat.

"No, please don't go… *Ooh*," The rest of her sentence was garbled and one long cry as he immediately went back to work, loving her.

He knew she referred to his lovemaking, but he planned to show her, in detail, that he was never going away again. This was his woman. And he was going to do everything in his power to let her know how much he needed her.

Lifting her bottom in the air, high, he brought her center to his mouth and swiftly, smoothly, stabbed her heat, suckling her deep into his mouth, immediately lost in the glorious scent, taste and feel of her.

The orgasm began low in Sonia's belly, rolling and crashing in on her in one glorious tidal wave, on and on and on….

Her body shot up, eyes open as she stared down at the dark head buried between her thighs.

"Oh God, oh God, oh God, oh God," she cried,

her body no longer hers to control, yet the reality that she was not dreaming beating against her, just as the incredible orgasm was.

"How…" She stopped, panting. Drew in a breath. "Why, wha—" Her incoherent babbling was cut short when his long, thick fingers stroked into her heat at the same time that talented tongue circled and hollowed, suckling her clit into his mouth with a sweet ferocity that was nearly painful in its intensity.

When his finger slanted deep inside her channel, he slowly, oh, so slowly released her clit, and the orgasm she thought was over swelled and crested, nearly drowning her in its intensity.

She fell back on the bed, allowing the incredible sensations to simply…devour her.

When he applied direct pressure right above her mons, his fingers still playing her, his mouth opened wide and clamped down over her entire center, and she screamed.

The orgasm broke completely free when he lifted her bottom high in the air and continued his sensual assault.

The feel of his tongue, teeth and fingers against her aching sex in alternating sensual strikes was her undoing. Her body went up in flames.

As she crested the peak and she felt unable to give any more, her spread her lips and added yet another finger.

"No, no, no," she babbled and begged, the pleasure too intense for coherent speech. *"Baby."* Her strident cry ended in one long wail of release and her entire body slumped down on the soft mattress, every bone in her body useless.

She kept her eyes closed, allowing her body to calm. Eventually she felt her heart return to a beat that didn't make her afraid she was in the throes of a heart attack, yet she was too sleepy, too listless… too satisfied to open her eyes.

"We're not done, baby." Key's deep-voiced pronouncement brought Sonia back to full wakefulness. She inhaled deeply and opened her eyes.

Her eyes roamed over his beloved features one by one. Although it was dark, the light from the moon the only light, she could make out his features. But she really needed to see him. There could be no mistakes this time.

Memories of how badly she'd misjudged the situation with him once before echoing in the recesses of her mind.

She slowly rose, scooting up on the bed until her head hit the padded headboard.

"I think…I think we need to talk first, Key," she began, her eyes scanning his face for any signs of residual anger…mistrust. A mistrust she knew she had every right to see. But one that if she did see, if he still felt that way, she knew that despite the good sex, their sexual chemistry would do nothing for them in the terms of a relationship. She wanted it all.

"Home. I want to go home," she whispered.

"Is that what you want, Sonia?"

Chapter 23

His question brought her up short, and her gaze flew to his. She hadn't realized she'd spoken aloud. She swallowed the lump of anxiety down. Embarrassed, yes, yet she knew it was all on the line now. They were past the getting-to-know-you stage. Way past that.

The fact that he knew what she meant by saying she wanted to go home confirmed what she already knew—that they were on the same wavelength as well as the same path. Fate had decided that long before they'd ever met.

And after all they'd been through, honesty was the only way to go. No more hiding away, not for either of them.

She tugged the sheet up on her body and forced

herself to keep his gaze. "I won't settle for anything else, and if that's not what you want, I'm okay with that. But if you want a relationship, I won't be happy with anything, Key, but the real thing."

A small smile played around his sexy lips, and she felt her heart skip a beat. Yet his next words brought her up short. "You know that just about killed me when I thought you had betrayed my family… betrayed the trust we were developing." He spoke bluntly, straight to the point, and although his voice was low, modulated, Sonia heard the catch in it and felt her heart react at what she knew was pain.

Did he still mistrust her? After what they had just shared?

She kept her eyes shut, afraid of what would be reflected in them should she look his way. Silently she nodded, waiting for him to continue. Maybe that had been his way of saying goodbye, she thought, squaring her shoulders and preparing for whatever he had to say.

She couldn't stay there and take his anger. She couldn't take going through the pain she had endured over the past two weeks. She felt indignant. She was not going to wait for him to lower the boom.

"Been there, done that. Got the heartache ribbon to go with it," she said aloud, and gathered the sheet around her body.

She turned to face him, tears running down her face. "Look, I know I was the cause for your father having to go to the hospital, and that is something

I will never, ever, forgive myself for. If he had..."
She allowed the sentence to dangle, not wanting to
put voice to the fear.

"I would have never forgiven myself for the pain
it would have caused you and your family. I don't
know what else to say. If you still don't believe I had
nothing to do with it, there's no point in any of this.
I—I only came back to speak to your family and
give a personal apology on behalf of the studio for
what Patricia did."

She turned, with tears clouding her vision, to
leave, not sure where she was going, only knowing
that she had to get out of the cabin before she completely lost it and broke down. She ran toward the
door, grabbing her clothes along the way.

"Wait, damn it, woman!" he shouted, close behind her. When he grabbed her by the waist and
lifted her, turning her around to face him, his face
was red with anger.

"Just where do you think you're going?" he de-
manded as he held her by her waist, suspended in
air inches from his face.

"I let you get away from me once, and that was
enough," he said, and lifted her higher, throwing her
over his shoulder and spinning back around.

He swatted her on the backside and she yelped
in surprise.

"What the hell was that for?"

"Never again will you leave me," he said, and
tapped her bottom again. She squirmed against

him. The swats weren't hard enough to hurt, but hard enough that she felt their slight sting against her sheet-covered bottom. Embarrassed, she felt her body react and had to clench her legs together.

He swatted her a third time, this one softer, his hand caressing the slight sting. She moaned against the sweet sting.

"And never again will you leave me alone," he said, and turned with her, laying her on the bed.

"You said that one already," she said, staring up at him. Her breath caught at what she saw in his light blue eyes, the sheen of tears too real, the stamp of emotion so raw on his face it brought an answering emotion.

She swallowed and said nothing. She couldn't say anything. She waited for him to continue.

He sat next to her on the bed, slowly unwrapping the linen from her body. With his voice neutral, stripped of emotion, he began to speak.

"After you left, I went and talked with my father and my brother. Although the shock wasn't good for my father, it wasn't the reason for the infarction. He didn't suffer a second stroke, just what the doctors called an infarction," he began, and she drew in a breath, guilt washing over her anew.

He drew her close, hugging her body to his. "It wasn't your fault, Sonia. I know that Patricia was behind it all. After you left, we pieced it all together."

"But if you didn't think it was me, why did you let

me think you blamed me? Why didn't you tell me?"
she asked, pain in her voice

Key drew in a breath.

That was a question he'd asked himself, one both
his brother and father had asked. He was man enough
to admit the real reason for accusing her of the betrayal.

"I was afraid." He made the admission, his jaw
tightening.

Afraid of what?

"Damn, baby, this isn't easy for me. I was afraid
of this…us, what it meant."

"I'm not following," she replied, her voice an-
guished and low, and he knew it was now or never.
He had to tell her what he felt, how much she meant
to him.

"I love you, Sonia. I've loved you for so long, it's
as though I loved you before we even met," he said,
and knew she heard the catch in his voice. "With the
first volley of emails between us, I knew you were a
woman to be reckoned with."

He stopped, a bittersweet smile on his face. "In a
lot of ways you're like my mother. Strong, indepen-
dent. Capable," he said. "I started to like you even
then, though I fought the show, fearing what it would
do to the ranch. The notoriety I could deal with, but
once I knew the true legacy of Nick's parentage, and
mine, I knew I had to protect more than the Kealoha
Ranch. I had to protect my family."

"And that's why you started being nice to me?" she asked in a low whisper. He heard the hurt in her voice.

"Sweetheart, if you recall, there wasn't any-thing...*nice*...about some of the things we did," he said, and laughed lightly when his comment met a fiery blush.

He bent down to kiss her softly on the top of her head.

"I told myself it was to see what you knew, what you and your crew were up to, but I wanted more than that. The show had nothing to do with how I felt, even if I didn't want to admit it to myself. At first I thought I'd get you out of my system while mak-ing sure you were on my side, just in case you did know my family's secret. But I was only fooling my-self. You were already under my skin by then. And it scared the shit out of me," he admitted frankly.

She leaned away from him to catch his gaze. "Why?" she asked softly, her eyes locked with his.

He drew in a breath.

"Because I was scared as hell you couldn't pos-sibly love me half as much as I was head over heels in love with you," he finished, and covered her sur-prised mouth with his.

He broke the kiss and placed both hands along-side her face, staring intently into her eyes. "I don't deserve you, baby, but, God, I love you, Sonia. I love you more than anyone or anything in this world," he said, his voice breaking as he saw tears falling down her eyes.

He felt an unexpected emotional tug and the sting of tears in his own eyes at her reaction.

His gaze took all of her in, from the sheet now loosened, hanging around her waist, to her curly mop of hair, gathered into a haphazard knot on top of her head, wild strands sticking out everywhere. She wore no makeup, and her eyes were tinged red from tears.

To him, she was the most beautiful woman he'd ever seen. And she was his.

"Please tell me you forgive me, baby. Please," he said, burying his face in the hollow of her throat.

He knew she had to love him. It was in her face, had been in her face for him to see. He'd been so damn stupid, refusing to admit what both his father and brother already knew. Not only did he love her, was crazy about her, she felt the same way about him.

She had every right to tell him to go to hell after the way he'd treated her, what he'd accused her of. And if she did, he'd keep right on loving her, until she admitted what he already knew.

He held on to her and waited. Her body's reaction to his also alerted him to the fact that she loved him. He felt the stab of her sweet nipples against his bared chest. He released a heartfelt groan of relief when he felt her small arms wrap around his neck.

He sought the nirvana of her lips before he forced himself away.

"I'm sorry, baby. So sorry… Please tell me that

you forgive me," he begged. When she nodded her head almost shyly, he felt a rush of relief.

Unceremoniously he flipped her body so that she lay beneath him on the bed, and he laid siege to her mouth. Between muffled kisses and intimate sighs, he murmured against the sweetness of her lips.

"I don't know how long I can last, baby. It's been so damn long and I've missed you so damn much, I ache," he admitted freely.

"I've missed you just as much, Key…now shut up and make love to me, boy," she quipped, and he laughed lightly along with her. All laughter came to a halt when he slipped a hand between them, slipping his fingers past the nest of curls at the juncture of her thighs and testing her readiness for him.

He lifted his finger and brought the evidence of her readiness to her attention. Keeping his eyes on hers, he licked her cream from his finger.

"Oh, God, baby, please make love to me," Sonia begged, and Key laughed roughly.

He tried to be gentle, knowing that in his rush he might hurt her. But he was as randy as he'd ever been and hoped for the best. Guiding himself to the center of her vagina, he carefully fed her small inches of his shaft, nearly coming when her walls clamped down tight on his cock.

"Easy baby, it's been a while," he said, his voice rough, low.

Closing his eyes, he clenched his jaw and pushed

swiftly, embedding himself inside her until he felt his sac tap against the seam of her butt.

Home. He felt as if he was home.

Making love with Sonia made him complete.

After adjusting her on him for their mutual pleasure he slowly began to rock inside her body, holding on to her hips as he made love to her. Although impatient, he wanted to make it last.

Wanted to make up for mistrusting her.

He wanted to relish and treasure her.

When he felt her wrap her legs around his hips, he knew that she had given in to the pleasure and was giving as good as she got.

"I've missed this, baby. But, God, I missed you even more.

"Oh, yes, Key...I missed you...missed this," Sonia cried as he stroked deep inside her willing body. Realizing he was holding back, feeding her *just* enough of his thick cock to tease she placed her hands on his hard, muscled butt and squeezed.

Not enough to hurt.

Just enough to feel good.

He shouted, his stroke picking up with deadly intent.

"That's what I'm talking about." She laughed, her body on fire from the heat of his touch.

"Oh, yeah...you like it rough, do you?" he asked, grinning at her, sweat dripping down his face as he continued his deep strokes.

"Hmm," she said, tightening her hold on him. "Just enough to feel good, Key," she said, and shifteded one of her hands below his butt.

"Oh, God, baby, where'd you learn that?" he asked, his shout so loud she was afraid anyone who happened to be within one hundred feet of the cabin would hear him.

She smiled up at him, her body on fire and the strength of his strokes making coherent thought a soon-to-be-impossible thing.

"Only from you, baby, only from you," she whispered, love in her eyes as she stared up at her man.

Her words made him pause fractionally and glance down at her before he continued. What she saw in their light blue depths told her more than mere words could ever tell her. He loved her.

"I love you, Key!" she cried out, her orgasm sweeping over her.

As she allowed the tide to sweep and engulf her, she heard him shout at the same time, declaring his love for her again.

With two more corkscrew thrusts, she felt his seed burst inside her body, and she closed her eyes, welcoming him inside her as together they climbed the summit and went over, reaching their peak in unison.

"Do you love me enough to marry me, Sonia?"

Sonia's eyes opened slowly before she shut them quickly, the sunlight from the cracks in the blinds blazing directly into her face.

She turned to face Key to find him intently watching her, one big leg thrown over hers as their bodies lay close together.

He toyed with one of her long curls, twirling it around his finger.

"Did you hear me, Sonia?" he asked, and although he said it nonchalantly, she heard the tension in his voice.

For some reason his nervousness acted as a calming agent for her. She smiled.

"You might as well give in and say yes. I'm not letting you out of this bed—off this ranch, until you do," he said, and she opened one eye to peek at him.

"Yeah, is that a fact?" she asked, keeping the laughter out of her voice.

"Damn right it's a fact. We'll just have to figure out the mechanics of it all. I'm not trying to take away your career—"

"Oh, thanks, that's a relief," she murmured, biting the inside of her cheek to stop herself from laughing.

"But I figure with you producing the second season of the show, you'll be here for another six months—"

"You all want to do another season?" she asked, astonished.

"I can travel back to L.A. with you during the off-season of the ranch. Nick can cover for me."

"There's an off-season for ranching?" she asked, but he continued to ignore her, outlining his plan.

"I can use the time to buy cattle from a couple of

the auctions in that area. I figure between that and you taking time off, we can make this work," he finished. If she didn't know better, she would swear Key was nervous.

Which made no sense, as he was the epitome of Mr. Cool. Her smile grew brighter.

Taking pity on him, she stopped him.

She grabbed him by his broad shoulders and brought his face down to hers to lay a kiss on his perfect mouth.

"I have news to tell you. I wasn't sure you would care before, but now…" She trailed off and told him of the new show she would be producing in the fall, as well as the new venture she had with her friend Dee Dee, a venture that would keep her in the field of producing, just from a different angle. Screen writing.

"Between the new show and the script, I'm going to be kept busy for a good long time," she said.

When she saw his face darken, she frowned. "What? I—I thought you'd be happy. And this way we don't have to film on the ranch anymore."

"But I don't mind. And I want you to know I trust you. You'll never believe I do, Sonia. That will always be something between us. Besides, why would you not want to do another season? The show is a success and it's all because of you."

"Key, I do believe you. My decision not to continue on with the show is because I know how much you value your privacy," she began, and when he opened his mouth to protest, she kissed him softly.

The kiss grew until she forced her lips away.

"And I don't want anyone invading my privacy, either," she said simply.

"But what about your career?"

She smiled. "My career will be just fine. I'm ready for change, and with the new show taping in Hawaii, I'll keep my hand in producing! This new venture with Dee Dee is one I've wanted to do for a long time."

"Well, now that you've shared your news, I have something to share with you," he said, and filled Sonia in on his phone meeting with Nate Wilde, the adopted son of Key and Nick's biological father.

By the end of his telling, she was in front of him, listening carefully.

"And Nick…how did he take it?" she asked, as he'd told her of Nick's not-so-great reaction to the news of who they were.

"He still isn't taking the news very well. He doesn't want to blame Dad, and he can't bring himself to blame Mom," he said, and she heard the frustration in his voice. "Seems he's hell bent on blaming someone. Unfortunately those someones are the Wildes."

He turned her around to face him and brought their faces together so that he could kiss her.

"I'm sure we'll figure it all out," Key said.

She smiled. "Together. Because that's what family does," she said, a shy smile coming out, exposing the tiny dimple in her cheek.

Key groaned. "What did I ever do to deserve you?"

"I don't know. But whatever it was, I hope it never goes away."

"No chance of that," he replied, and was about to kiss her when he realized she hadn't answered his question.

"Well?"

She didn't have to ask what he meant. A grin lit her face.

"Yes, Key, yes, yes, yes, yes, I'll marry you," she promised, and squealed when he grabbed her and hugged her tightly to his body, releasing a loud whoop.

"Time to seal the deal," he said, a purely masculine light entering his bright blue eyes.

He caught her mouth with his in a kiss that brought a flush of heat coursing through her entire body. As she moaned into his kiss, welcoming the weight of his body on top of hers, her last thought was that the kiss wasn't the only thing to seal the deal.

The deal, their fate, had been sealed the first moment they'd spoken. Before they'd ever met, fate had sealed the deal.

Now, forever and always.

* * * * *

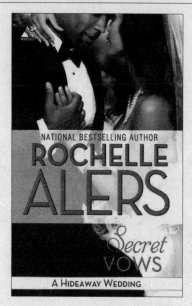

REQUEST YOUR FREE BOOKS!

2 FREE NOVELS
PLUS 2 FREE GIFTS!

KIMANI™
ROMANCE

Love's ultimate destination!

YES! Please send me 2 FREE Harlequin® Kimani™ Romance novels and my 2 FREE gifts (gifts are worth about $10). After receiving them, if I don't wish to receive any more books, I can return the shipping statement marked "cancel." If I don't cancel, I will receive 4 brand-new novels every month and be billed just $5.19 per book in the U.S. or $5.74 per book in Canada. That's a savings of at least 20% off the cover price. It's quite a bargain! Shipping and handling is just 50¢ per book in the U.S. and 75¢ per book in Canada.* I understand that accepting the 2 free books and gifts places me under no obligation to buy anything. I can always return a shipment and cancel at any time. Even if I never buy another book, the two free books and gifts are mine to keep forever.

168/368 XDN F4XC

Name _____ (PLEASE PRINT) _____

Address _____ Apt. #

City _____ State/Prov. _____ Zip/Postal Code

Signature (if under 18, a parent or guardian must sign)

Mail to the **Harlequin® Reader Service:**
IN U.S.A.: P.O. Box 1867, Buffalo, NY 14240-1867
IN CANADA: P.O. Box 609, Fort Erie, Ontario L2A 5X3

Want to try two free books from another line?
Call 1-800-873-8635 or visit www.ReaderService.com.

* Terms and prices subject to change without notice. Prices do not include applicable taxes. Sales tax applicable in N.Y. Canadian residents will be charged applicable taxes. Offer not valid in Quebec. This offer is limited to one order per household. Not valid for current subscribers to Harlequin® Kimani™ Romance books. All orders subject to credit approval. Credit or debit balances in a customer's account(s) may be offset by any other outstanding balance owed by or to the customer. Please allow 4 to 6 weeks for delivery. Offer available while quantities last.

Your Privacy—The Harlequin® Reader Service is committed to protecting your privacy. Our Privacy Policy is available online at www.ReaderService.com or upon request from the Harlequin Reader Service.

We make a portion of our mailing list available to reputable third parties that offer products we believe may interest you. If you prefer that we not exchange your name with third parties, or if you wish to clarify or modify your communication preferences, please visit us at www.ReaderService.com/consumerschoice or write to us at Harlequin Reader Service Preference Service, P.O. Box 9062, Buffalo, NY 14269. Include your complete name and address.

KROM13R